The Prime of Miss Jane Austen

By

Lisa L. Jorgensen

www.ThePrimeofMissJaneAusten.com

WHITE STORK
BOOKS

ISBN: 978-0-9859476-3-7

Cover portrait of Jane Austen reproduced by permission of Paula Byrne.

Chapter 1

It is a truth universally acknowledged that a single woman in want of a good fortune must marry well.

"The journey alone must be quite shocking," said Cassandra, passing the soup to Mrs. Austen. "How Tom will bear it, I cannot conceive."

"But, my dear, it is too late now," said Mrs. Austen. "Tom is a healthy and sensible young man, and will certainly come back with a ready living in Shropshire. Only think of your future. The year will run quickly enough, my dear."

After a spoonful of soup, Mrs. Austen thought to add, "*My* health, you know, could never support such a journey, even at Tom's age. To be in such an uncivilized country! Whatever would there be to eat? And how I would suffer in the heat! I would be quite unequal to it, I can assure you."

"And yet, Mamma," said Jane, "there are thousands of young men in the West Indies. Tom will not be a regular soldier, you know. He will not be in real danger. His circumstances will be as good as Lord Craven's, who will surely be as attentive to Tom as may be. Pray, let us hear no more on that score when we have our own Cassandra for but one more year before she leaves us."

"Quite right, my dear," said Mr. Austen,

touching a napkin to his lips. "Providence will steer the course of young love as it will. There is a certain derring-do in young Tom that I admire, I daresay. And now's the time for it. Your lives will be long enough, if God wishes it, for Tom's service abroad to be but a brief interruption of your courtship."

"And we have so much to do in the way of your wedding clothes, to which I do not think you have given proper thought, my dear," consoled Mrs. Austen, leaning towards Cassandra. "You have been so very agreeable and patient in all respects towards Tom that you've neglected your own mother's feelings. Every mother, you know, longs for the day she can advise her daughter on matters of matrimony, and on seeing her finally out of the house. It will be the happiest day of my life, I can tell you," she said with a satisfied smile.

On this unsettled ground, supper was concluded in the Austen household on the eve of Cassandra's leave-taking to Kintbury at Christmas time in 1795. She was to stay with the Fowle family to say farewell to Tom, her fiancé of two years, before he left for the West Indies as chaplain to Lord Craven's regiment. Having taken holy orders a few years prior, Tom had still not found a living sufficient to marry. Luckily, Lord Craven, Mrs. Fowle's wealthy cousin, had several livings in the surrounding area to bestow, one of which Tom hoped for as a reward for his time well served.

Mr. Austen had himself only been able to marry when he was offered the living of the village of Steventon some twenty-one years earlier. As the rector now of both Steventon and neighboring Deane, he was gratified that Cassandra, his oldest daughter, was to marry a clergyman. This was particularly so since, as a gentleman without independent fortune, Mr. Austen was able to provide neither substantial dowries nor inheritances for his daughters. And Tom Fowle was a particular favorite to join the family, not only because of his personal qualities, but because he had been one of the family since he was a boy. He had been a pupil of Mr. Austen's in the early years when the Austens took in student boarders to supplement their income. He had been a fine and devout student with an exemplary character, a boy whom everyone could love.

Of the Austen daughters, Cassandra was the most even-tempered. That she would become an excellent wife and mother could be doubted by no one, for she had long been a mother to her sister Jane, two years younger. Mrs. Austen, though energetic and charming in her earlier years, had had but little time for her girls. She had six sons to raise and to see off into the world in addition to four or five other boys boarding as students in the house. Now with much less to do since the boys had grown, she took to quarreling with the servants and taking colds as often as possible.

Jane and Cassandra became all the more inseparable, with that fortunate balance of constitutions found in the happiest of marriages. If

Jane went too far afield towards impertinence, Cassandra raised her eyebrows and cautioned. And if Cassandra was in a somber mood, Jane devised elaborate stories, sometimes stretching over entire days, abusing all their ill-natured relatives and neighbors. Anyone who might be passing the rectory on fine days, in fact, would likely see the two young women in their every-day bonnets and long muslin dresses and shawls, Jane the taller, walking through the garden and into the surrounding lanes in the midst of deep intrigues of Jane's invention.

Jane took to writing some of these stories in her brown writing book, disguising characters' names in such a way that only she and Cassandra would know their true identities. The stories were later read aloud to her family, for all the Austens loved the opposition of reason and passion, especially foolish passion.

These stories and peals of laughter constituted many evenings by the glowing fireside of the old stone rectory.

Chapter 2

A light snow had fallen overnight, but it was not sufficient to delay Cassandra's trip to Kintbury. Rather, it lent a glittering look to the landscape in the morning sun. John, the Austen's manservant, was to drive Cassandra the entire way. After breakfast, as the carriage was loaded with bundles and gifts for the Fowle family, the Austens were more solicitous than usual when one of the family traveled.

"Take care, my dear, to relate our sincere prayers for God's watchfulness over Tom and Lord Craven. And remember that the family will be no less sorry to see Tom leave than you. Turn your sorrow into service to your new family, then. And write to us often. Whatever we may do for them, we shall do, you may be sure," Mr. Austen said at the doorway.

"I am only sorry that we cannot do more, but we have only two jars of strawberry jam left after the three you are taking," said Mrs. Austen, shielding her eyes from the brightness. "The strawberries have not been as plentiful this year, you know. I have thought of late to remove the strawberries to the beds at the side of the house. They may like the light better there.

"Jane, there is a project for you in spring! John will be only too glad to turn the soil when it thaws," Mrs. Austen assured her.

"And I remind you, Cassandra, to always wear your woolen stockings to bed. I will not be held responsible if a cold catches up to you if you do not. There is no telling what manner of drafts and ill-built fireplaces and thin counterpanes the Fowles may have. I would not risk such uncertainties without stockings to bed for all the world. Indeed, I would not."

Jane and Cassandra exchanged glances, as they often did when their mother prattled on. They loved their mother dearly, but were painfully aware of her foolishness and propensity to maneuver conversations towards herself.

"I am always sorry to see you go," said Jane to Cassandra when the carriage was ready at last. "It will be dreary here until you return. But I shall write to you every day. Or every other day, to be sure. Three days at the very least. And you are to see Tom this evening!"

"Oh, I know not whether to be happy or to grieve that he will be leaving a few weeks hence."

"Then I shall tell you, if you do not know."

At last, Jane was left to wave until the carriage disappeared around the curve of the lane. Although it was a chilly morning, Jane walked a little around the gardens, looking like miniature snowy hills, and to the back where the pigs and chickens were as noisy as ever. She wrapped her shawl closer. How different Cassandra's life would be than hers, she thought. To be married! To have children! That is where the cycle begins and ends. Perhaps that's all there is, really. Have our lives served God's purpose when we have procreated? How dreary. And, as if it were not sufficient for childbirth to signify the end of a woman's worth, it often brought death, as well, to emphasize the point.

For her own life, the matter was uncertain. She tended one day towards marriage and a respectable life, and the next towards...she knew not what. Certainly love. There must be love. But to risk one's life in childbirth was a grim bargain. Children or death. Perhaps children *and* death. Unlucky, indeed.

She stamped her short boots on the raised threshold at the back door, hung her brown bonnet on its hook, shook out her short brown curls, and slipped quietly into the dining room to avoid being discovered. Jane was a quick sort of person generally, quick of mind, quick of judgment, quick of movement, and quick of temper. The foibles of her family and acquaintances, and even of herself, seldom went unnoticed.

She sat down at the window table where she liked to write. It was circular and small, but it was just the right height, and she particularly liked its compactness. A larger table might have encouraged her to stray too far from her plots, to meander and lose her momentum, and to allow too many characters into her world. Yes, it was precisely the right size.

When the rest of the house was quiet, as it was now, and when she was bent over her writing, she was as fully absorbed in her world as if she were reading. In fact, if she had been asked why she wrote, she would have said that it was because then she could later read exactly what she liked. Since no one else had taken that trouble, the task had been left to her.

She lifted up the writing box that she kept next to the table. In it was the manuscript *Elinor and Marianne*, the first real novel she had written. Though her reciting of it had been met with general approbation by her family, she owned that the epistolary style used to good effect in her short novel, *Lady Susan*, had been perhaps stretched beyond its limits, and may no longer be in fashion. She tied the manuscript now with a ribbon to remind herself to allow it to rest after months of scratchings and crossings out.

Her former writings had been the diversions of a girl with an active faculty for small stories and wit. But now, the dear Dashwoods, having once been created, continued their lives in ways that were difficult to leave behind in her writing box. They continued on without her—their marriages, their children, their lives in the village. Imaginary lives, to be sure, but they would be lived.

Were this novel to be published, she thought, the Dashwoods would be out in the real world, and perhaps be loved by more than just herself. That was worth consideration. Having a few extra coins in her pocket was appealing, as well. But the notoriety to herself and to her family would be unseemly, however diverting the idea. For the present, it would be enough to allow the Dashwoods their privacy.

She closed her writing box, and looked out the window for some time with her chin propped up on her left hand. All those people in their carriages. What were their circumstances? Were they to visit some odious relatives only because they might be mentioned in their will? And then later discover that they had been slighted in favor of some other odious relatives? Or, were they the odious ones? Some of them certainly looked as though they might be, she thought. Proud, in any case.

Chapter 3

Several weeks later, the first of the winter balls was to be held at Ashe Park, the grand residence of Mr. and Mrs. John Portal. With Cassandra away at the Fowles', Jane was left with her own taste in front of the small mirror on her bedroom wall. She had planned for days to wear her rose gown because she had been complimented by how well the color complemented her complexion. But, laying it on her bed on the afternoon of the ball, she was disappointed in it, and felt that it was in need of something, she knew not what. She lay on brighter ribbon instead of the lace. She tried a different sash and a different necklace, imagining how they would look on her. But nothing would do. Everyone would have seen them all before in every configuration she could devise. At last, she threw the dress over her shoulder, and went in search of her mother.

She found her downstairs in the pantry, scolding Cook for eating the last bit of gooseberry pie—a favorite of Mrs. Austen's.

"Oh, Jane, what a fuss about your dress! No one will notice in the least. And why should they? There are to be new visitors. Do not flatter yourself that you are the only girl who grieves at a paltry wardrobe in advance of a ball. It is the hallmark of every young lady catching beaux to try to outshine even her particular friends. But, however, now I think of it, I have laid by a pretty sort of flowered satin that may do very well. Molly! Fetch me the flowered satin from my cupboard."

"Ah, does it not look well?" asked Mrs. Austen when the article was produced. "It does not take much, you see, to turn a turnip into a turban."

Although the comparison of her rose gown to a turnip without the flowered satin was vexing, Jane could admit that with the flowered satin, the gown looked very well. She did not often find success in appealing to her mother for advice. Mrs. Austen had a peculiar gift with words, as apt to offend by thoughtlessness or unfortunate constructions as to provide relief — and often simultaneously. In this instance, however, Jane was much too pleased with the result to make a complaint about either the turnip or trying to outshine her friends.

When the carriage was brought round after supper, the Austen party, consisting of Jane, her older brother James, who had come home for a visit, and Mr. and Mrs. George Austen, were searching for gloves and a hat and a muffler for one or the other of them. John, the driver, gave a wink to Molly, who was nearly beside herself with all the commands Mrs. Austen had been issuing about the preparations. Only Mr. Austen was as composed as usual. His nature was to be always prompt, but, weighing that ideal against the turmoil that would ensue if even the smallest item were left behind, his nature also allowed for expediency.

"Oh, how I love a ball! What more could one

hope for than everyone at their worst behavior?" asked Jane of James when they were on their way at last, the light snow crunching beneath the wheels. "But, *you* must not be ill behaved, James. You must do your part in searching out anyone in need of a partner—particularly me. I was mortified at the last ball to be without a partner for four dances together."

"Had I been there," said he, "I would have favored you above anyone."

"You are all goodness, James. And, your dancing has improved vastly with my tutoring this last week. I shall claim all the credit for any conquests you make this evening."

"Be assured, then, that if I do make any conquests, you shall have the credit of them all."

"It shall be no less than I deserve."

Mr. and Mrs. Austen, being accustomed to these repartees from their children, especially from Jane, took no notice of them.

Chapter 4

Here was a scene coming into view to gladden the heart. Every window at Ashe Park shone golden. Coachmen assisted arriving parties up the gravel walk through the snow towards the welcoming open door, and stable boys saw to the horses. This scene gave particular pleasure to Jane, as she rather liked the hubbub of servants, the barking of dogs, the impatient hoofing and neighing of horses, the commands of gentlemen, and, most of all, the general discomfiture of ladies forced to endure the elements outside their own homes and hedges. She would have preferred to delay her own entrance to witness this scene longer, had not her own mother exhibited just that sort of peevishness.

"Oh, my dear Mr. Austen, how unlucky for us is all this snow," she said.

"The horses, I believe, must have more reason to find inconvenience of it," answered he.

"How can you be so tiresome, sir? A good two inches of the hem of my gown will likely be utterly ruined."

"It is fortunate, then, that your general beauty and charms must fix everyone's gaze above your hem for the entire evening, my dear. I fear the horses can have no such consolation."

Oh, my own dear papa, smiled Jane.

"Absurd, Mr. Austen! James, where are you? Give me your arm, if you please. Your father cannot be applied to for assistance, for he is unnaturally occupied with the happiness of the horses."

"I do confess a general sympathy for beasts of burden," said Mr. Austen, but these words were lost in the forward motion of arriving guests towards the grand entrance of the manor.

The scene inside was one of guests being relieved of their outer wraps, and accommodating themselves to the warmth. One such guest, the Reverend William Heathcote, had not only shaken off the evening chill, but was in some danger of wilting his stiff collar with discomposure at being slighted by Miss Elizabeth Bigg.

Although Elizabeth was the oldest of the Bigg sisters, she was not inclined to marry merely because Heathcote found himself in readiness. Contrary to the Austen girls, the Bigg sisters were at perfect liberty to marry or not to marry, as they chose. Their father owned the grand estate of Manydown Park, and had, therefore, no pressing requirement to look to sons-in-law for his girls' fortunes. At their ages of twenty-two, twenty, and eighteen, not only were all three of them out in society at once, they usually attended balls together, severely straining the delicate balance of eligible males to females at these gatherings. Of the three, the youngest, Alethea, was plain and shy. But Catherine, or Kitty, who was Jane's particular friend, and Lizzy were both elegant and charming.

"Oh, Mr. Lefroy! We have looked forward to making your acquaintance ever since your arrival at

Ashe Rectory. How very quiet you must find our little village compared to your Dublin," Lizzy gushed.

"Just so, and delightfully so, I assure you," he beamed. "It gives one pause to simultaneously reflect and plan. The last few years have been taken up with studies and busyness of every sort. How good it is now to be back in nature and draw an honest breath."

Thomas Langlois Lefroy had recently set an outstanding academic record at Dublin's Trinity College, and meant to pursue the law in London under the sponsorship of his great-uncle, Benjamin Langlois. The two-month-long visit to Ashe Rectory of this illustrious nephew with unbounded prospects was an event producing no small degree of pride for Tom's uncle, the Reverend George Lefroy and Madam Anne Lefroy. Nor had there been a moment of disappointment since his arrival, for he was a gentleman in every regard, and ready to be pleased in every circumstance, in addition to being so fortunate as to be handsome. The rumor of this last point had preceded Tom to the ball, and was uniformly confirmed by every female attending.

The hired musicians were beginning to tune their fiddles and flutes, which signaled the time to begin the fine diplomacy of gentlemen seeking dance partners, and women gambling on whom to accept and whom to avoid or outright decline. Declining was the absolute last resort since one could not accept another request from anyone later without seeming to insult the former.

"I do love a country dance, Miss Bigg. May I have the honor of the first two dances with you?" Tom was in unusually high spirits. After almost a month spent indoors with his uncle and aunt and their young daughters, he had vowed to enjoy himself as much as possible during this second month. His time to be serious again in London in studying the law would come soon enough.

"I would be delighted, sir," said Lizzy, having narrowly avoided the same request from the approaching Heathcote. To deflect his mild embarrassment of being outdone, Heathcote turned to ask the same of the nearest female he could find: a smiling Miss Jane Austen.

"I would be delighted, sir," said Jane, noting at the same time out of the corner of her eye that the new visitor with whom Lizzy was to dance wore just the sort of expression and smile that she could wish every young man should attempt to attain, if he possibly could. And there was something sparkling in the eyes.

"What do you hear from your sister, Miss Austen?" inquired Heathcote between the back and forth of the country dance. "How does she find Kintbury?"

"Oh, her letters are as cheerful as she herself is. She describes the country as being almost as charming as Steventon, and Mr. and Mrs. Fowle are as attentive and kind as if she were their own daughter. I would not deprive her of one moment's pleasure with Tom Fowle before he departs, but I do confess that I miss her a great deal, and wish her to return as soon as possible. I am not proud of this failing in me, but neither can I deny it."

"The love of a dear sister, Miss Austen, is reason enough to miss her. God cannot find failing in that, surely. But, she must live her destiny, as you must live yours."

"Do you believe in destiny, then, sir?"

"I believe that God has a destiny for each of us, yes. We know of it first as a calling, I believe, an awareness of a purpose in life, what we are made for. My calling has been to spiritual service, and I was fortunate enough to feel it early in life. Many others struggle mightily in their lives when their calling eludes them. Have you not observed it?"

"Indeed, sir. Indeed," she answered distractedly.

Her mind was occupied elsewhere. Down the dance line on the opposite side was Thomas Lefroy, and Jane found no room for any other thoughts than of him at the moment.

When the dancers at last retired to the furniture, Lizzy found Jane, and introduced Thomas Lefroy to her.

"Miss Austen, at last I have the pleasure," he said with a bow. "My aunt has spoken so very highly of you these last weeks, I could scarce believe such a person existed."

"You flatter me, Mr. Lefroy. A sensible reply

to such an exclamation is quite impossible. I can only offer my hope that your disappointment shall not be excessive. Mrs. Lefroy is all goodness. I have admired her these many years, and I have been so fortunate as to count her among my friends."

Heathcote was now at Lizzy's side again with renewed hopes of securing her for a set of dances. Alas, she could no longer escape the offer.

However, the remainder of the evening belonged to Tom and Jane, at least as they would each remember it in later years. To dance together did not occur to them until they had filled each other with opinions of books and music, nature and God, and family and friends. Jane was particularly engaged by Tom having a sharp sense of humor, similar to her own. It was a quality Jane's family was amused by well enough at home, but which had the power of mortifying them when she displayed it elsewhere.

"Nothing is more enchanting in a gentleman than an Irish brogue, I believe. However do you manage it, Mr. Lefroy?" asked Jane.

"Ahhh, as with most social affectations, it comes by continual practice. You may be sure that I speak quite normally when out of public hearing."

"It is just as I suspected, sir," laughed Jane. "It cannot be possible to think or speak for very long in another language. It must simply be too exhausting."

"And yet you see the happy result before you. I believe you used the word "enchanting," did you not, Miss Austen?"

Oh, what a Tom, thought Jane. Such wit, such manners, such gentlemanly good looks.

The banter flew back and forth, hardly diminishing even while they danced later in the evening. A little game developed whereby they took turns besting each other at wit upon approaching each other during the dances. And when all other topics seemed spent, they began abusing the general company.

"If this dance does not end soon, there will be at least one gentleman whose toupee will be sliding down sideways. Have you spotted him yet?" asked Jane.

"Oh, I die a little at every turn he undertakes. He cannot be sensible of how precarious are the nerves of everyone on his behalf."

In short, the ball was a success. Whether it would have been more or less of a success had the toupee lost its moorings could only be conjectured.

On the drive home, Mrs. Austen expressed approbation of the manner in which Heathcote and Lizzy had danced and behaved themselves in general.

"That is what I call good manners," said she. "How is it possible, Jane, that you should embarrass your family even further than at the last ball? Mr. Austen and I despair of your ever securing a respectable husband. Have you no regard for the ridicule of your neighbors? And with me catching a cold with all this snow. Really, it is too bad."

"But for what do we live, Mamma, but to provide sport for our neighbors, and to laugh at them in our turn? I believe I may say that I shocked no one within their hearing. James, do take my part. Were you shocked by my behavior?"

"I should say not! I was, however, occupied elsewhere conducting my own conquests, and so saw nothing of it. But, had I actually seen your behavior, you may be certain that I would not have been shocked in the least."

Chapter 5

"It is bad enough to flirt as unashamedly as you did with Tom Lefroy, Jane. What I cannot forgive, however, is that you left so little opportunity for anyone else to have their chance," said Lizzy the next day. "You must know that I admired him myself."

"But what could I do? Only consider. Mr. Lefroy was at liberty to choose his partners as he wished. I cannot speak for his taste, Lizzy. But, I can certainly admire it!" laughed Jane.

"As it was, I was left in a continual state of avoidance of Mr. Heathcote. His persistence is most vexing," said Lizzy.

"I do admire *his* taste, as well," said Jane. "But, that is not surprising since you are almost five times the beauty of anyone in the neighborhood. As for me, surely you cannot hold a resentment for long of someone as much your inferior as I am."

"Indeed, I do wonder at it. He must have been told of my family's fortune by his uncle; how it could be to his advantage in securing his future."

"Do not despair of it, Lizzy. There are to be more balls. I hereby give you my word that I will leave Tom Lefroy at liberty for at least five minutes together at each one. There, that's generosity for you, is it not? And then you may make your best mark. Are we friends again?"

"I hope we shall always be friends, Jane. I

could not bear it otherwise. But what shall I do with poor Heathcote? Can you not take him off my hands? That is what I would call real friendship. As a clergyman, he is much more your sort. How I wish to spend the season in London, instead. But with so many girls in the family, my father is not inclined to undertake the adventure or to leave the younger ones behind. What am I to do?"

Catherine, the middle sister and Jane's best friend, now entered the garden path where Jane and Lizzy were walking.

"Oh, there you are, Jane. I had heard you were come. How do you do this morning after your wild evening?"

"I'm astonished, Catherine, that you would call it wild. How can you abuse me so, especially since you would not take the trouble to be there yourself?"

"My love of the sport of dancing is not nearly as passionate as yours seems to be. Balls exist primarily to torment the lovelorn. If I am to be a spinster, I will accept my fate as well as possible, and without an audience to confirm it to the world. But now, Jane, is it true that you amazed the whole room with your frantic lovemaking with Mr. Tom Lefroy? Can you deny it?" asked Catherine.

"Who says so? Of course I deny it! I was absolutely not frantic at any time. But, oh, what a gentleman he is! Amiable, amusing, clever, handsome! I wish you had been there. He is everything a gentleman should be, is he not, Lizzy?"

"How can you torture me by encouraging my compliments of him?" complained Lizzy. "Yes, he was as lively and charming as any I have known. More's the pity, for I think he shall make a name for himself some day without me!"

"And without you, as well, Catherine," said Jane. "For I claim him for myself, and I hope that he will have the goodness to abide by it. There, it is settled. And you shall see for yourself, Catherine, at the next ball, which you cannot escape, for it is to be here at Manydown."

Turning to Lizzy, Jane said, "And you have no cause to object, in any case. Dear Mr. Heathcote is so very attentive to you."

"Oh, he is, but I had hoped for better than a clergyman. A baronet would be much more suitable. A handsome one, and one with a little mystery, you know. Mr. Heathcote is so very predictable, so sensible and upright. Tom Lefroy is much more interesting."

"But, alas, no fortune or rank, Lizzy. Quite unsuitable," said Jane.

The garden path led them back to Manydown now, where Harris, Lizzy's and Catherine's younger brother, waited for them.

"W-w-where have you been all this t-t-time?" he said, stamping his rather large boot on the gravel, reminding Jane of a drawing Cassandra had made as a child of a large rabbit thumping his hind leg.

Harris, at fourteen, was the unfortunate heir

of a family of fortune. His stammer could, perhaps, be overlooked, were it not for his rather ungainly posture. Like a tall sapling in the wind, he seemed perpetually off balance. He had grown in height over the past year to such a degree that he tended to bend at the top, looming as he approached them.

"My f-f-father wishes to see you, Catherine. I daresay you are in for it, for he has d-d-discovered his Plutarch on your writing table."

"Oh, dear. I only meant to borrow it for a few hours. But how did he discover it to be missing in so short a time? What had you to do with this, Harris?"

"Oh, he only noticed that there was a g-g-gap on the bookshelf, and asked me if I remembered what book it was. When I said I believed it was the P-P-Plutarch, he suspected that I knew of its whereabouts. Rather than having him suspect that I had taken it, I hinted to him that it c-c-could have been in someone's bed chamber. He found it in yours, that is all."

"And how was it that you knew what book it was? Were you in my bed chamber?" asked Catherine.

"D-d-do not be so hasty. I only surmised who may have borrowed it. You are the r-r-reader in the family, after all. In any case, he wishes to s-s-speak with you directly."

Chapter 6

"We are fortunate, are we not, my dear, in our little community of country families?" observed Reverend Lefroy. "As I looked out from the pulpit last evening at the earnest, upturned countenances of our neighbors, hopeful of a new year of health and grace and prosperity, it seemed to me that the blessing was all mine, most assuredly; that I was entrusted to guide them towards happiness for yet another year. It swells my heart to think of it. What a pleasure now to see everyone in merrymaking!"

Madam Lefroy could scarcely hear the reflections of her husband above the general noise of the ball. For Manydown House was now quite full of red-cheeked gentlemen in vests and tights, and of ladies in enough fabrics and fripperies to overpower them. A stout holiday punch and generous cold supper on the sideboard did not fail to further encourage the gaiety of the party.

"Quite fortunate, indeed," said Madam Lefroy. "As for the new year, we have every reason for optimism. Only consider our fine crop of young men and women, ready for marriage and families of their own. That is the sort of prosperity that makes *my* heart swell."

The community was indeed fortunate, not least due to Madam Lefroy herself. Amiability and brightness of mind, together with a sharp perception of human nature, made her a welcome guest at every occasion. Jane, in particular, was fortunate in her companionship, especially when Cassandra was away from home. For Madam Lefroy enjoyed discussing books and ideas with her as her own mother did not, indeed could not, and was as capable of delighting in wicked nonsense as Jane was. In addition, she flattered herself to be the foremost matchmaker in the community, which never failed to amuse Jane.

"There are two worthy creatures, in particular, just now whom I would wish to see well married, my dear: Miss Jane Austen and Mr. Lovelace Bigg-Wither," said Madam Lefroy to her husband. "Were they only of an age, the matter would be easy enough: he has the fortune, and she has the brilliancy. Advantageous as it would appear, however, inheriting a widower with eight children, some of whom are her own age, would render poor Jane bereft of any privacy of thought or deed for the rest of her life. It would most likely shorten it, I daresay. No, no, it cannot be thought of."

"Nor have they likely thought of it themselves, my dear," replied Mr. Lefroy. "These matters must take their own course, you know."

"Nonsense. Family and friends must take a part in directing their gazes. For they themselves are invariably short-sighted and incapable of judging which partner is most likely to provide lasting happiness.

"There, you see Jane before you," she continued. "She has but one fault: a girlish attraction to the handsomest young man in the room. And so charming is she that she engages him easily, leaving him quite incapable of thinking of any other young woman. I fear our Tom is quite smitten."

"But that cannot be, madam," said Mr. Lefroy. "He is the hope of his entire family to raise them up. Uncle Benjamin would certainly not look upon such a hindrance to Tom's education with approbation, especially not with a village clergyman's daughter without fortune or family connections."

Uncle Benjamin Langlois was the patriarch of the Langlois Lefroy family who had undertaken sponsorship of Tom's education.

"You take my point entirely, sir," said Madam Lefroy. "Matters must *not* take their own course if we can but guide them. I will encourage Jane to turn her attentions elsewhere. And you must speak with Tom on the matter. If he is to stay with us for another two weeks and two more balls, we cannot entirely prevent them from meeting and dancing."

"If I remember rightly, madam, the last ball is to be at our own rectory, is it not? Can we not at least delay that ball another week, when Tom will have gone to London?"

"Yes, certainly, if you wish it," said Madam Lefroy. "But, it would be at the expense of the others not to have their merriment during these dreary days. Let us first see how this evening advances before we undertake a decision."

Just then, an uprising in the crowd broke the dancing into disarray, and the small group of musicians stopped their playing and turned their heads towards the commotion. Several gentlemen were seen to be assisting a lady into a chair.

"Madam, you are quite overcome. Lizzy, fetch the smelling salts directly. Is there anything I can provide of assistance? Shall I escort you to the parlor? What can be done?" inquired Lovelace Bigg-Wither, the master of the house.

"Oh, oh," cried Mrs. Harwood. "More punch, if you please. I fear I am dying. It is the cream puff, to be sure. It has been poisoned!" she said in a swoon.

"Poisoned? Poisoned? Surely not, madam. What can you mean by it?"

Most of the party had now gathered closer, to the varying degrees their good breeding permitted.

"I tell you I am dying, of thirst at the very least, sir. More punch. Make haste, or I shall expire!"

While others tended to Mrs. Harwood's requests for more punch, Mr. Bigg-Wither picked up the offending cream puff. Quite aside from his alarm at Mrs. Harwood's sudden attack, he was also surprised that the cream puffs, his cook's pride and joy, were called into question. His cook had been with the house long before his wife's death some ten years previous. Never had she failed to satisfy in every respect, being highly meticulous in managing the kitchen and foodstuffs. But now that he peered into the cream puff, he noticed that the cream filling was not its usual color of pale creamy yellow. It was very nearly brown.

"What can be the meaning of this? Catherine, take this tray of cream puffs away to Cook at once. She is to meet me in the parlor directly with an explanation of them," he ordered.

With Mrs. Harwood seeming to recover her wits, even at the expense of her sobriety, Mr. Bigg-Wither proceeded to the parlor, and waited for the confrontation.

"Sir, I am all in a dither!" cried Cook. "Someone has filled a half dozen of the cream puffs with brown mustard! Upon my word, I cannot account for it."

"Mustard? How can it be possible? Was there anyone else in the kitchen?"

"I cannot think, sir. Oh, dear. There was the delivery boy this morning at the kitchen door. But he could not have come near the cream puffs. Quite impossible, for they had not yet been made."

"Who else, then? Think, woman."

"I can think of no one, sir. Indeed, I cannot. Master Harris came through a little earlier, of course, to try a few of the cold meats, but that is not unusual. He is a growing boy, after all, and always has an appetite, bless him."

Mr. Bigg-Wither's color rose from a mild pink to a ruddy red at the same time that his eyes grew big enough to alarm her.

Master Harris was promptly discovered in the ballroom with a face as red as his father's, and laughing heartily within a small group. A few minutes later, everyone in the group except Jane had managed to stifle their laughter as young Harris was hurried up the stairs by his father close behind.

"He is simply too horrid for words, Jane," said Catherine. "Look, Mrs. Harwood is on her feet again, but see how she staggers. Poor unlucky woman."

"She may be unlucky this evening, but it may well be *Mr.* Harwood's luckiest night, do you not think?" laughed Jane.

"Oh, how you seek out the wicked," said Lizzy.

"It is what I live for, I assure you," said Jane.

"What is that? What is it you live for, Jane?" asked James Austen, just joining the group.

"Why for Mr. Tom Lefroy. No one else will do," she teased. This was bolder than she had intended, being in a silly humor by Harris' prank.

"In that case, I need not doubt that you will do me the honor of accepting the next two dances with me," said Tom, rescuing her from embarrassment.

"I fear I have diminished the air of mystery I have so long sought to cultivate. I cannot think how to recoup its loss," said Jane.

"But that does not signify since the object of it has already been achieved. I stand before you at your service," said Tom, leading her to the dance floor.

Never had this extent of open flirtation been experienced in Steventon. There was no shortage of raised eyebrows to be seen among the company, nor of wagging tongues, none of which escaped the notice of Mr. and Mrs. Lefroy or of Mr. and Mrs. Austen.

"Is there to be no end of spectacles this evening?" asked Lizzy to James. "I'm mortified in my own home, and cannot escape it."

"But none of the spectacles are to your discredit. You are therefore quite at liberty to laugh at them with everyone else," said James.

"Certainly not. It would be insupportable for me to sink to the level of these jesters. I have no wish to join in that sort of merriment."

"Ah, I quite understand you. Yours is a more serious nature, is it not?"

"I hope so. As the oldest child of my dear father, I feel it my duty to uphold the dignity of his name and home. And, although my father's estate will inevitably pass to Harris, it will be many years hence until Harris can manage it, if ever. I feel it most sincerely," said Lizzy.

So encompassed in this thought was Lizzy, that she did not see Heathcote advancing.

"Are you unwell, Lizzy? You look quite pale," said he.

"It seems our Lizzy is dismayed by all the silliness this evening. You and I must join forces to raise her spirits," said James. "What do you propose?"

With this, Lizzy's heart sank even further in anticipation that Heathcote would propose yet another set of dances. And dancing would only force her to exert herself with more smiles.

"I propose merely to allow Lizzy her own wishes. You take much upon yourself, you know, Lizzy. I would by no means wish to add to your burdens. But I pray you would seek me out if you wish to take a walk in the garden."

Chapter 7

"This is just the sort of exercise to encourage the bloom of health in your cheeks, Mamma," said Jane, walking briskly with her mother on a lane towards Ashe Rectory. "There is very little snow, and it is scarce two miles."

"Quite excessive, my dear. I can't think how I could have been persuaded to undertake it. My poor legs and heart are all atrembling. I can only hope that the Lefroys will have the goodness to drive us home again. This is too much to be borne. If I do not catch cold, it will be quite a miracle. And if I do, it will be at your insistence."

"But, Mamma, it was so irregular for Tom not to pay us a visit after the last ball, I fear he may have become ill. Or, indeed, Madam Lefroy herself may have done, or Mr. Lefroy. Or the entire family! Only think, Mamma! Why, we should be thought heartless by the entire neighborhood," said Jane. "And I could not undertake the walk alone since Tom will most likely be in attendance. It would be unseemly, would it not, to arrive unchaperoned."

"You will, indeed, be unchaperoned if I faint away before we arrive," cried Mrs. Austen. "And if the Lefroys are not all prostrate in their beds, I shall have exhausted myself for no good reason whatever."

At last, Ashe Rectory came into view. Mrs. Lefroy, having seen them approach from the parlor window, came to the door, herself, to welcome her visitors.

"Oh, my dears, you are very welcome! And such a cold day, bless me. Pray, come and sit down, sit down. I hope you have not brought troubling news. Your family is not ill, I hope," said Madam Lefroy.

"Oh, no indeed. We are come to inquire after yours," said Mrs. Austen. "We cannot think what may have prevented young Tom from paying a complimentary visit to Jane after last Friday's ball. He was so very good in attending to those little courtesies, you know, after the previous ball. Naturally, we despaired of something being amiss, that perhaps he lay ill, or that you had all been taken by a putrid fever, or worse."

"Why, nothing of the kind, Mrs. Austen," said Madam Lefroy, not a little surprised. "How very extraordinary that you should think so. We are all in splendid health. Mr. Lefroy and I did mention to Tom how very attentive he was to you, Jane, and whether you may not prefer at the next ball to have more opportunity to be available to other young gentlemen. It may well be that Tom wished to avoid seeming too forward in seeing you again so soon. In any case, he meant no discourtesy. Quite the contrary, for he speaks so very highly of you, my dear.

"Well, so long as you have come so far," she continued, "let me entreat Tom now to pay his civilities. He was just here reading a book."

"Oh, pray do not trouble yourself, madam, or Tom," said Jane. "Do not suppose we came here to seek a courtesy from him."

But, this was exactly what Jane had come for. Or, at least, she was hoping to see him again. She was now ashamed of herself. She saw now how obvious her plan was, and Madam Lefroy was so kind in indulging her that it made Jane even more ashamed. Tom would see through her plan, too. But there was no means of escape now.

"Not at all. Not at all. Tom will be very glad to see you. Lucas, pray ask master Tom to come to the parlor," said Madam Lefroy.

But Tom was nowhere to be found, thereby putting the final touch on Jane's mortification.

Chapter 8

"I have been advised by my uncle and aunt that I would do well to create less of a scandal for the neighbors," said Tom with a wink at Jane at the following week's ball at Deane House, home of the Harwoods.

"Then let the scandal be all mine," said Jane, seeking to deflect her embarrassment. "Lizzy, Mr. Heathcote, will you not take a walk with us?"

Among the estate's splendors was a vast greenhouse used for wintering over delicate plants. To encourage admirers, Mrs. Harwood had directed that the greenhouse be lit up with candles and oil pots of every kind, the flames of which doubled their charms when reflected upon the glass panes. The resulting effect was of a fairyland against the dark night.

"You may consider these lights all in your honor, Tom," said Jane as the party entered the greenhouse, "to wish you a very happy birthday. As it happens, today is my sister Cassandra's birthday, as well, so you see, we are almost of a family."

This remark was not lost on Lizzy, who would have preferred to exchange walking partners had she not comprehended the futility of encouraging a gentleman of such meager fortune. She rolled her eyes with a smile towards Heathcote, whose own inclination thereby led him to hope that Lizzy might regard *him* as almost of *her* family.

"Why, that is just the sort of talk we have been warned against," laughed Tom.

"Perhaps you have, but I never have, nor do I bend easily to attempts at intimidation," said Jane. "As I am nearly a month older than you, I shall set the example that you may profit from it."

"But, I fear my aunt and uncle must hold sway since they are my hosts and guardians," said Tom more seriously. "I beg you will not think the lesser of me."

"Indeed, I cannot. Your other qualifications do you sufficient credit. Any gentleman who admires Fielding's *Tom Jones* cannot be all bad. Or all good, for that matter," laughed Jane.

For the remainder of the evening, Tom and Jane danced only one set, but they spent considerable time sitting down together and walking around the rooms. It was during this time, on this evening, on Tom's birthday, that Jane fell in love.

So, this is what it feels like, she thought while riding home in the carriage that evening. There's a sort of affirmation and knowingness that had been lacking with mere infatuation. Heathcote had been right about destinies, she thought. Here is mine.

Chapter 9

"I can assure you, Uncle, I shall have matters well in hand this evening regarding Miss Austen," said Tom to Mr. Lefroy. "Do not imagine me insensible of the future of my family. I feel it sincerely. Not only am I deeply in your debt and in Great Uncle Benjamin's debt for sponsoring my law studies, I am, in truth, quite ready to undertake them."

Mr. Lefroy was, with this assurance, able to smile.

"There is no one in whom my faith in the future could more confidently be placed than with you, Tom. And, you shall go far, I daresay. Your personal qualities together with your academic achievements bespeak the makings of greatness. I am certain of it."

"You honor me, sir. In truth, both my heart and my mind are called to the law. I am determined to dedicate myself to the betterment of not only my own family, but to Ireland, immodest as that may sound. My studies there did not hide from me the iniquities of its laws and society," said Tom.

"May I suggest to you that your success will depend, in no small part, on your ability to immerse yourself wholly into that life," added Madam Lefroy. "Without encumbrances, I mean, at least for the next few years."

"Indeed, Aunt, I have not the least intention

of encumbering myself," said Tom. "Ah, are you perhaps referring to my intentions regarding Miss Austen?" he continued. "I hope I have given no false expectations there. She is, undoubtedly, one of the most remarkable young ladies of my acquaintance. There are not many whom I so much admire for their wit, their understanding, their affability. And, yet, we must remain as we are: friends."

"Forgive my impertinence in asking, but you have not, then, given her an offer of marriage? Or an expectation, or an understanding?" asked Madam Lefroy.

"I have not."

"I am much relieved to hear you say so," said Mr. Lefroy, "for your sake, as well as for hers. You seem well suited in every respect except that of fortune. You have yet to command yours, and she can provide none of her own. Better that she should find a husband of means, and that you should remain unencumbered, at least until you are called to the bar.

"Added to these considerations is the matter of which country in which to reside. You are determined to return to Ireland, and Jane's friends and family are all here in England. Only think how cut off she would be. For my part, I doubt not that, after an acquaintance of only a few weeks, you will have forgotten each other in as many weeks hence."

Chapter 10

The evening brought a slippery mixture of snow and sleet to the narrow lanes, making travel to the Ashe Rectory for the fourth ball an exercise in apprehension, not least of which to Jane, who had already spent the day in anxiety. This was to be Tom's last ball since he would be leaving for London within the week.

She had written to Cassandra the day before, "I look forward with great expectation to this ball, as I rather expect to receive an offer from my friend in the course of the evening." This had been written half in jest, but not wholly in jest.

But today, she could be sure of nothing, writing, "At last the day has come on which I am to flirt my last with Tom Lefroy, and when you receive this, it will be over. My tears flow as I write at the melancholy idea."

"Catherine, I hope I may count on your assistance this evening, as I fully expect to expire of dread," said Jane that evening.

"Why, I hope you may always be assured of me. Are you really so very apprehensive?"

"I cannot recall a time of greater confusion mixed with excitement and I know not what. My feelings, I can barely account for them. They may well overtake my sensibilities if I do not take care. Oh, how am I to survive this evening?"

"In matters such as this, I believe the best

remedy is a bowl of punch to settle one's nerves. Stay close, and I shall guide you," said Catherine, moving easily through the dining room.

Tom Lefroy had not yet come down from his bed chamber, for he had apprehensions of his own. All that he had said to his uncle and aunt earlier in the day was quite true. He had not given Jane an offer of marriage, nor any expectation of it.

He wondered now, however, whether he had implied anything of the sort. Had he behaved less than honorably? Did all the dancing and sitting down together and teasing lead Jane to believe that he admired her above all others? He had no friends to help him put order to his confusion. His only certainty was that he did, indeed, prefer Jane above all others.

He at last descended the stairs, determined to behave in a gentlemanly manner. He moved first towards his aunt and uncle, who seemed relieved at his presence and his composure. And then he was quite on his own to make of this last ball the best that he could.

Mr. Heathcote could always be relied upon to provide comfort wherever it was needed. Catherine had, therefore, beseeched him to occupy and distract Jane this evening, if it were possible. That seemed particularly unlikely to almost everyone in the room, however. They had watched Jane and Tom's flirtations and attentiveness to one another over the course of these four weeks. The two of them had been the subject of many little titters and surmises as they gossiped in the lanes and shops.

"Your sister returns to Steventon next week, I believe. You must be most desirous of seeing her again," said Heathcote to Jane.

"With all my heart. She is my conscience, you know, in all matters, and I rely on her good judgment when my own falters. My hope is that she may arrive before Tom Lefroy leaves for London, so she may see for herself whether or no he is the finest young Irishman she has ever beheld."

"No one who has met him could think otherwise. He is everything a young man ought to be. Do you remember that we spoke of destiny several weeks ago? Tom Lefroy has that good fortune of seeing his before him. He appears to know he is made for the law, and has pursued his studies with determination to that end. He is much to be admired."

"No one in this room could admire him more than I do myself, I daresay," she said.

"His future success will depend, in no small measure, upon his willingness to delay, and even forgo, the ordinary distractions of a young man for the next few years. In that, we may encourage him," said Heathcote, hoping his hint was not too overbearing.

"You are referring to his delaying an attachment, I suppose. Certainly he should. On that score, all who wish him well must agree. The burden of a family of his own would be much too great to consider."

A sense of relief flooded over Heathcote, who had been charged to take the measure of Jane's affection for and expectation of Tom Lefroy. He could now report to Catherine and Lizzy that Jane perfectly understood the wisdom of allowing Tom to proceed to London unfettered. The three of them, therefore, perceived no real danger when Tom descended the stairs.

Madam Lefroy was the next to intercept Jane, for she was also desirous of reducing Jane's and Tom's time together. The fondest of mothers (for so she almost was to Jane) and the best of friends, she could not bear the prospect of seeing Jane hurt.

Eventually, of course, Jane's and Tom's eyes met, and both knew that this last evening could not pass without some talking and at least a little flirting.

Tom brought her to a small sofa which could hold only two, for he did not wish to be overheard. Having been supplied with two bowls of punch by Catherine, Jane was now no longer in any danger of the dread she had feared.

She was most anxious for Tom to speak first, to broach the subject both of them had skirted until now. But, after a few minutes of silence, she surmised that he may need some small encouragement.

"How quickly these weeks have passed, Tom. I would say that it seems just yesterday when we first became acquainted, but that would belie how much we have come to know one another. What is your opinion? Have the weeks passed quickly?"

"Since my visit started a full month before you and I met, my experience of time passing is different from yours. I would say it has been just about right. I would not have missed any of this time for all the world. You have all become quite dear to me, and always will be."

Tom was able to look directly at Jane for the first part of this exclamation, but not for the second. Had he said too much?

Again, Jane waited, for it seemed to her that a declaration was imminent. But, again, he needed prompting.

"We have become quite accustomed to seeing you at these balls. I, for one, shall miss our acquaintance. Exceedingly. Have you any plan of returning?"

"I fear my plans are not in my power to control since this marks the first time I will be reading law in London. I may well be called home to Ireland if any holidays are permitted."

"Oh, they must be! And there may be shorter breaks in your studies that may enable you to come to Steventon, or rather, to Ashe. Do you not think it likely?"

"I'm afraid I have not inquired about holidays, as yet. I have been so very grateful and indebted just to be able to attend the lectures and to have a sponsor in my great-uncle Benjamin."

"To be sure. But, we are not so very far away, after all. You will write to your uncle and aunt, I suppose."

"Oh, without fail. They have become quite my own family. I am very attached to their girls, and certainly hope to see them as often as possible. Well, I see that we have many eyes upon us, Jane. Shall we give them a dance? May I have the honor?"

He was now able to face her directly again with a smile, having come through his trial with success. Jane's trial was also apparent on her face, but it did not reflect success. In his haste, Tom did not see the brief welling of her eyes.

The end of the evening saw them together once more, as all wished Tom the very best in his travels and studies. There were hearty handshakes all around, and to Jane he bowed and smiled sweetly, which he could now afford to do. "I am much obliged to you, Jane, for these very charming weeks of dancing and what-not. I hope you will remain close friends with my uncle and aunt. Au revoir, then."

The next morning was the best time, in the opinion of Madam Lefroy, for Mr. Lefroy to drive Tom to London. His behavior at the ball had given no one cause for alarm or embarrassment, and yet his countenance was somber enough at the end of the evening that she thought it wisest to avoid the possibility of Tom wandering towards Steventon or of Jane wandering towards Ashe during the week. Or worse, of them both wandering towards the middle.

"Well, and there's an end to it," said Madam Lefroy to Mr. Lefroy. "They will both very soon recover to normalcy, and no harm done."

Chapter 11

"Cassandra! Oh, how good it is to see you, you cannot conceive," cried Jane as Cassandra's carriage drew up to Steventon Rectory. "But you look so altered. Has it really only been a month?" asked Jane as Cassandra stepped down from the carriage.

"Jane! But it is you who have changed. If it were possible, I should say your cheeks are twice as rosy as before. Surely not on my account."

"Oh, entirely on your account! But now you mention it, there is so much to say that I dared not mention in my letters for fear you would be reading them aloud to the Fowles. I am in excessive want of your good sense, of which I have less every day."

"Jane, can you not see that Cassandra is exhausted?" said Mrs. Austen, as Cassandra entered the front door. "I suppose that the Fowles neglected to give you any provisions for your journey. No little sandwiches or cakes, such as I like to prepare for travelers. I have found a general decline in what I call good breeding. Not only on the part of the Fowles, but even in good families. It is sad to say, but there it is."

"But, Mamma, you see no little sandwiches and sweets because I have eaten them all. Mrs. Fowle and her cook have been most attentive, and made for me the most wonderful provisions. Oh, this package is for you, Mamma, with a little note."

"It is remarkably well written, my dear," admitted Mrs. Austen. "Better than I could have expected. Oh, look, girls. We shall have cakes for the entire week. Very pretty. Very pretty, indeed. And, you know, this is a testament to how much the Fowles admire you, Cassandra. The note speaks very highly of you, and of how pleased they were that you were able to come to them, and so on and so forth. Of course they were. There. Very gratifying, indeed."

In fact, Mrs. Austen's gratification was such as to be sufficient for the remainder of the evening. Therefore, as Mr. Austen was away attending to parishioners, Jane and Cassandra retired early to their bed chamber.

"I can have no secrets from you, Cassandra," said Jane, who sat on her bed while Cassandra unpacked her things on her own bed. "I must own that I am violently in love. Now I know what you have been feeling for your own Tom."

"But do you not think that every love is unique, and that it changes?" asked Cassandra. "When my Tom first made his declaration, the sensations were new to me, too. There was gratitude, to be sure, and great joy. Joy for both the present and for the future. But with the dreams and plans he and I have made, my love for him has altered. It has become deeper and richer so that he is a very real part of me. It is difficult to know now where I leave off and he begins within my own soul."

"Were you never really so in love, then?"

"I was certainly not as prodigious a flirt as you are, for one thing," she said with a smile. "Really, Jane, you astonished me. Mother has written how mortified she has been with your behavior, and how the neighborhood has become a teeming cluster of gossips. How can you support such behavior?"

This was not the path Jane had hoped her first conversation with Cassandra would take. Jane was past being admonished. She had traversed all the way towards despair. All her efforts at securing Tom Lefroy had been for naught.

"I have thought of little else since he has removed to London," said Jane, more somberly. "We were only to have a few weeks, a few balls, together. How I wish you could have come home sooner to meet him yourself.

"But, I am not mistaken, Cassandra. I know he loves me. We had so little time that I tried to make the most of what we had in order to encourage him."

"And, did he make the most of *his* time? Did he make visits to you between the balls?"

"Not as often as I could have wished. Oh, do not make me think he does not care for me. My heart is already broken."

"My dear Jane," comforted Cassandra, now close to tears as Jane already was. "You mistake me. I meant only that it may be too soon to know his true intentions. He may wish to take more time because he will be away, and he has his studies to consider. Do you expect that he will return? What were his words to you?"

"I shall never forget them. He said that he would continue writing to his uncle and aunt Lefroy. And his last words to me were "Au revoir," which means that he plans to return to me, does it not? These words are all I can live for now," said Jane. She could not hope for letters from Tom, in any case. Unmarried ladies and gentlemen were permitted to communicate only through guardians, perhaps to avoid them ruining their lives by planning to elope.

In her misery, Jane had not asked Cassandra about the Fowles, her trip, the particulars of Tom Fowle's leave-taking, or how well she was supporting herself through her difficulty. Cassandra was, in fact, sufficiently stoic to manage her emotions well. Nor did she begrudge Jane's lack of inquiry, for she knew that Jane did not have parents like the Fowles to share her thoughts with.

Jane's emotions, for her part, were much less organized. She grieved deeply for the loss of Tom Lefroy, and for his not making a declaration despite of all she had hoped for. And, not least, that Cassandra had already been engaged at her age.

"It seems to me that our destinies are not so different," said Cassandra at last. "We are destined to wait for our Toms to return. In that we may comfort each other."

Chapter 12

"What a letter from Tom this morning, my dear," said Mr. Lefroy. "He writes that he leaves for Dublin next week. His studies are on hiatus until November, and he is dismayed that he has been unable to interest Uncle Benjamin in meeting any of the Austens, including Jane. Benjamin remains adamant that a penniless clergyman's daughter must not distract Tom from being the hope of his family. It would seem that our expectation that Tom would have forgotten Jane by now has not come to pass. Perhaps there is more attachment than we imagined."

"What can be done, my dear? We could invite Tom here, but I expect he does not wish it. His heart may break again, as may Jane's, if there really is an attachment," said Madam Lefroy. "I can think of nothing we can do now on their behalf. If Tom has been very persistent on the subject, Uncle Benjamin may well be quite weary of it. Time alone may still be the best remedy."

During these months, Madam Lefroy had been careful to avoid discussion of Tom whenever Jane came to visit, as she often did. Although Cassandra was certainly Jane's first confidant, Madam Lefroy was very engaging in matters of literature, history, and poetry, and was constantly active with amusing projects of one sort or another. And, as Ashe Rectory was only a few miles away, Jane also looked forward to the exercise through the summer fields and lanes on fine days .

The first opportunity Jane had for a much-needed change of scene was in August. Two of Jane's brothers, Edward and Frank, were to travel to Rowling House, Edward's home in Goodnestone village, and Jane was asked to accompany them to visit with Edward's wife Elizabeth and their children. As Jane was relating these plans, it occurred to Madam Lefroy that Uncle Benjamin might be persuaded, now that some time had passed since Tom had removed for the summer, to put the three Austens up for a night on their way through London. Both Mr. and Mrs. Lefroy thought this a particularly good time since Edward had just inherited vast estates from the Knight family. The Knights, having had no children of their own, had adopted Edward many years ago in order to have an heir. And now that he had come into this inheritance, Edward was extremely well provided for. Uncle Benjamin could well see this as favorable for Jane, and be more open to idea of Tom's attachment to her.

Frank's career in the navy was rising, as well, having been awarded a lieutenancy a few years ago. Uncle Benjamin could also judge the charms of Jane without Tom's presence, or even knowledge. It was Uncle Benjamin's decision, after all, whether he would support Tom's education if Tom were to become engaged to someone as penniless as Jane.

Enough time had passed since Tom had left for Dublin for the summer that Uncle Benjamin did grudgingly agree to this plan. He was, after all, a little curious about the family from all that had been related to him from Tom and now from his nephew. And if he still could not give his approbation of the family, Tom would never need to know of it. There seemed to be no harm in such an acquaintance.

Although Edward had become a somewhat proud and distant brother through his adoption by the wealthy Knight family, he was quite willing to make an effort to help Jane. And, Frank was eager to help on any occasion for the sake of his family. And so, it was arranged.

The three of them emerged from their carriage on Cork Street in London, and had their bags placed beside them in anticipation of being greeted presently by a servant, as they had announced their arrival to Uncle Benjamin by letter the day prior. When no such servant materialized, Frank pulled the door bell. After checking that they had the correct street number, Frank pulled the bell once more.

"What can be the meaning of this incivility?" asked Edward, who was used to better service.

"Good morning. You would be the Austens, I believe," said an elderly man-servant at last, opening the door just enough to allow the party through: Frank first, Edward second, and Jane last, bringing with her one of her bags.

"Surely we are not expected to retrieve our own bags," whispered Edward, just loudly enough to be heard by the servant. In spite of Jane's wish for everything to go easy, she could not restrain a small smile. Had it been happening to someone else, she would have whispered back, "Had we only known in advance, we might have brought our dog." This thought made her smile a little more, of which the servant, now passing out the door towards the bags, caught a glimpse.

"Francis Austen, sir, at your service," offered Frank heartily to Uncle Benjamin. "And this is my brother, Mr. Edward Austen Knight, and my sister, Miss Jane Austen. We are very much obliged to you for your kind offer of hospitality."

"Not at all, not at all. You are very welcome, I am sure. I hope your journey has not been an arduous one. We have cool weather today, which is a relief compared to the heat yesterday. Quite insufferable, you know."

"We have had a very pleasant journey, I thank you," said Edward, regaining his affability.

"I only hope we shall have no more of the heat. It tends to exhaust one, does it not, Miss Austen?" asked Uncle Benjamin.

"To be sure, it keeps one in a constant state of inelegance," said she, hoping Uncle Benjamin had at least a touch of good humor. Alas, he did not.

"For myself, I hope always to maintain a proper degree of elegance. I believe it is required of a gentleman of my station in life. For others, I cannot speak, of course."

With this subject now deflated, Uncle Benjamin began a long discourse on the merits of his extensive career, during which Jane was forced to let her bag down discreetly. He at last offered his guests a seat in the parlor, in which the heavy draperies were drawn almost together, throwing a gloom over the conversation.

After an hour of suffering through the one-sided opinions of this tedious man, Jane reached her limit. He had not given her a moment's opportunity to speak, and seemed disinterested in anything beyond his own position. She at last found an opportunity of inquiring whether she might be excused to rest from the journey. The servant soon appeared again, and escorted her upstairs to an equally somber bed chamber, where Jane soon collapsed in exasperation on the bed.

Edward now had an opening to speak a little on the subject of the Austens. He related the circumstances of all his family, and, in particular, how it came about that he had the good fortune to become favored by the childless Knight family, to be adopted by them, and to have inherited vast estates at Steventon, Chawton, and Godmersham. Frank, for his part, discussed his career in the British navy, of great import during these Napoleonic wars.

Uncle Benjamin now became quite animated and responsive; first, because a gentleman of vast property always interested him, and secondly, because talk of the navy provided yet another opportunity to mention his contributions to the glory of England.

"But tell me, gentlemen, of your sister Jane,

of whom I have heard much."

"She is the most delightful creature imaginable, sir," offered Frank. "She is goodness itself, and has a quick understanding and good sense. Quite accomplished, I may add, in writing and literature, and plays the piano beautifully. A true and faithful sister to us all, I can assure you."

"And what of her prospects, Edward?" asked Uncle Benjamin.

"Steventon, as you may imagine, sir, offers but a limited choice of suitable gentlemen for someone of her qualities. As she is of a retiring nature, well satisfied to be at home, we have not conceived of subjecting her to a full season of social activity at Bath or London, where, admittedly, her prospects might be improved. However, she often attends the local balls and assemblies in Basingstoke, which draws rather a better sort."

"And what are her expectations upon marriage, sir?" asked Uncle Benjamin.

"Why, nothing to speak of, sir. Our father is a clergyman, after all," admitted Edward.

"Pardon my mentioning it, but having inherited substantial means yourself, I wonder you have not considered providing for such a favored sister in order to secure a better future," said Uncle Benjamin.

This was as bold a confrontation as Edward had ever been subjected to, and it caught him quite unprepared.

"Our family's expectation, sir, is that Jane

will find her future from among the gentry whose fortunes do not absolutely depend upon those of his bride. In point of fact, my sister Cassandra is engaged to be married to the Reverend Thomas Fowle, whose expectations will likely be similar to our father's. I flatter myself that Jane may have at least the same good fortune."

In another point of fact, the idea of providing his sisters with dowries had been considered and rejected by Edward. At the time when Cassandra became engaged to be married several years ago, Edward had not yet come into his inheritance. During the intervening time, he saw no urgent need to supplement Cassandra's income since her future was already secured. To provide a dowry now for Jane would be to slight Cassandra in arrears. And, to provide them both with dowries seemed excessive. Hence, nothing had been done, and nothing was intended to be done.

"Come, come, sir. Let us not argue the point. I comprehend your meaning perfectly. You have a young family, yourself, and the maintenance of your properties must not be inconsiderable. We all must prioritize our resources, to be sure, and it seems clear that you have done so to your own satisfaction. Let us say no more on the matter."

Later, when alone in their bed chamber, Frank advised Edward that Uncle Benjamin had disapproved of his unwillingness to provide a substantial dowry for Jane, but Edward could not see it. He felt that the two gentlemen, being of similar stations in life, quite comprehended one another other and their responsibilities.

Shortly thereafter, Frank and Edward left Uncle Benjamin's house on separate business in London, leaving Jane to write a letter to Cassandra on their adventures, and to bide her time until the evening, when she and her brothers would escape to Astley's Amphitheatre for a horsemanship exhibition.

Nothing was said to Jane during their stay about Uncle Benjamin's confrontation with Edward. Frank felt it was kinder not to distress her, and Edward did not wish to think further upon the matter at all.

Chapter 13

"Truly bad. Hilariously bad. I could write a book with him as the only character," laughed Jane as she and Cassandra talked about the events of Cork Street when Jane returned to Steventon. "I so longed to write to you the full details, but I dared not. Neither Frank nor Edward thought him so very bad, but they are all kindness, you know. Frank has more patience than I do, certainly, and Edward has a way of not noticing what he does not care to notice.

"Uncle Benjamin, in any case, was much more pleased with himself than with his company. We stood standing for the first half hour of his discourse on his own consequence before it occurred to him to inquire if we cared for any refreshment after our journey, or even to be seated."

"Abominable! What could he mean by it?" asked Cassandra.

"Why, he meant to demonstrate his superiority, to be sure. But,Edward can perform with superiority quite well on his own, you know. What sport it was!"

"But what was the result, Jane? There was an objective, after all, of seeking his approbation of you," said Cassandra.

"As to that, I can assure you I did not misbehave, but neither was he willing to be charmed. Thank goodness he was unable to attend

Astley's with us that evening, or I would have come apart at the seams from restraint of laughing. He made us deep apologies, as if we had set our very hearts on his attendance, and sent us away in his best carriage, for he assured us he had several."

"But what of the next morning? How did you leave him?"

"As quickly as we could. His old servant had not at all improved from the day before, and gave us not the smallest hint of pleasantry. But, no matter. Uncle Benjamin was quite affable. He inquired into our remaining journey, bid us remember him to the Lefroys, and wished health and happiness to our families. He included Edward's family, I believe, as that subject had arisen the day before, as I comprehended later from Frank.

"Edward thanked him quite gallantly for his very kind hospitality, Frank expressed his warmest regards, and I said that I wished him pleasant weather, as a remembrance, you know, of our first meeting. I had hoped that he would offer a little smile, at last. But he would not. And then we were away."

"Did he speak of Tom, at least?"

"No, not at all, nor did I wish to bring Tom to mind. Uncle Benjamin and Tom are so very different to each other that they scarcely seem related."

"And yet, Tom's future is entirely in his gift," reminded Cassandra. "Surely, you cannot afford to be cavalier."

"No, certainly. But, as I have since considered it, unless Tom has learned courage from his hero, Fielding's Tom Jones, in being of true nature, he is less of the gentleman I have judged him to be, or less attached to me than I supposed. If Uncle Benjamin, after our efforts during our visit, will not give approbation of me, then Tom alone must decide our fate. Like you, I am perfectly willing to wait, if only Tom will come to Steventon to ask it of me.

"I do sympathize with how you must suffer during the wait for your own Tom, Cassandra. It must be miserable, I own. Do you find that it helps to dream a little, or at least to dream of your wedding clothes a little?"

Cassandra smiled easily. "Of course, it helps to dream. But what helps the most is to remain active and occupied, in which I hope I can set the example for you. I have helped mother this last month with her garden projects. She complains so bitterly about her stiff knees that I have at last arranged for a cushion to be placed close to the flower beds for her. I then have the pleasure of watching her waddling sideways on her knees, shifting her skirts and the cushion, and muttering in exasperation as she works. I have often thought of how you would be amused to see it."

"Indeed I would," Jane laughed. "You do have some of my wickedness, Cassandra, much as you deny it."

Chapter 14

"My dear, you must not spoil Molly so. *She* is to polish the silver. If you continue to do it, she will forget her duties altogether," said Mrs. Austen. "And, really, Cassandra, it is beneath you. We may not be wealthy, but we can certainly maintain our dignity."

"But these little tasks do help to pass the time, Mamma. I rather enjoy keeping house. And, knowing how these tasks are to be performed will help me teach servants in my own home."

"Oh, pish. How can you talk so? You are simply in want of mental stimulation. Learn to play the piano like Jane. No, no, that I would not wish, now that I think of it. One person is quite sufficient for my nerves. Go for a walk, then, to the Biggs. Or, go into the garden and sketch some flowers. Why have you no other interests, Cassandra? Have Mr. Austen and I raised you up to be a dullard?"

"I hope not, Mamma. It is raining, after all, and not fit to be outside."

The door creaked as Cassandra came into the dining room. Jane was just looking over the *Elinor and Marianne* manuscript again.

"Oh, I am glad it is you. I was just thinking how odd it is that I should miss Elinor and Marianne as if they were really my friends, practically my sisters. Now that I'm waiting for Tom to return, they're quite a comfort, really."

"How I wish I had your talent in writing. I cannot construct a story at all," said Cassandra.

"Well, then, you can help me with something, if you wish. But say nothing of it to anyone. Not to mother or father or to anyone. Do you swear it?" asked Jane.

"Of course I do. How can you suppose otherwise?"

"Well, in this case, it is particularly important. That is all I mean. I have in mind another book, you see, and I do not want mother asking me to read it before there is much to read. She nearly drove me to distraction with the last one.

"I have in mind that this new book will be in narrative form rather than epistolary, but I do not know if I can manage it."

"You did that before in earlier stories, quite successfully, I believe."

"But those were only stories. Now I wish to write about families and villages and all manner of characters over longer periods of time. Letters will do if there are only a few characters. Otherwise, the form is stretched past its limits, with everyone writing to everyone else. I foresee it would be either unmanageable or unreadable. What is your opinion?"

"I see what you mean. Of course, I have not given it any thought. Will it be a romance?"

"Most likely, but not at first. I beg you will not laugh or even smile when I tell you what I have in mind. I have been dreaming of what my future will be with Tom Lefroy. No smiling! He will be a great gentleman, of course, and quite wealthy. And he shall fall violently in love with me, and we shall marry after many turns and tricks, involving a great deal of family foolishness.

"But, I must take care to conceal the characters so as not to be evident that I am the authoress, much as I long for fame."

"Do you, Jane?"

"Certainly. Fortune, as well. And if not both, then fortune alone will do. I would not wish to embarrass my family by imprudent fame. However, it has not damaged Mary Wollstonecraft, to my knowledge."

"To the contrary, Jane. She has led a scandalous life, and eyebrows are raised in every home where her name is mentioned."

"But not because of her writing, and that is the main point. Writing by women may well be associated with an uncommon life, but that is only because uncommon women are the ones who dare to do it. The idea that women would have any ambition at all beyond the home is considered shocking because it has the power to threaten men's primacy, that is all."

This was the second time Jane had expressed this opinion since having read Mary Wollstonecraft's treatise *A Vindication of the Rights of Woman*. The first time was of an evening spent with Cassandra and their parents some months ago. Both parents were, indeed, shocked, although Mr. Austen had admitted there may be some truth in it. Having a scholarly interest in history, he did not question that it would be possible for women to have more consequence in the matters of commerce and the arts, he only questioned whether English society in particular would tolerate such freedoms.

"What nonsense, Jane," Mrs. Austen had said. "It is all very well for you to write for the amusement of your family, but pray do not suppose that it will be tolerated elsewhere. I should be mortified for our neighbors to be gossiping even more over you. I would be tempted never to speak to you again. I warn you not to put me to such a test."

"I will need to be careful to disguise all the characters," said Jane now to Cassandra. "What has particularly interested me is the relationship of Lizzy and Mr. Heathcote. He is one of the most interesting and dear people I know, and Lizzy is, too. But she is so very proud, you know, that her heart may never really be won by anyone without a fortune."

"I have asked Lizzy why she seems to avoid Mr. Heathcote when he is so very attentive to her," said Cassandra. "She said that she did find Mr. Heathcote charming and gentleman-like, and that she even found him to be handsome, in his way, but that she could never be satisfied with a husband who was inferior to her. In public, especially at balls and assemblies, she wishes to be appear completely unattached."

"She will lose him, if she does not take care, unless she changes her idea of inferiority," said Jane. "I rather like this as a theme. What say you to a change of gender? The proud, wealthy one could be the gentleman, and the charming woman could be the one without a fortune. This is all close enough to my own circumstance. I like it more and more."

She took out a new sheet of foolscap, and wrote "First Impressions" at the top.

Chapter 15

The winter passed with no word of Tom from Madam Lefroy, although Jane spent many hours in her company. The balls were insipid without Tom, and Jane despaired of him ever returning for her. But Cassandra was a wonder of hope and consolation and patience. Her quiet good humor distracted Jane when the wait for Tom seemed eternal.

"You do have the advantage of me in knowing that your Tom is returning, and that he is secured," said Jane one day. "I envy you that, I own. To be genuinely attached with no assurance of an understanding is what I find so vexing. Do you suppose there is more happiness in giving up all hope?"

"You ask more philosophy of me than I possess. But would you really be happy to be married with children of your own, Jane? You are not so very domestic. And, your husband may not approve of your writing. Nor would you be likely to have the time or the peace you require for it."

"I believe I would not marry at all if I could not write."

"Would you refuse Tom Lefroy, then, if he forbade it?"

"Oh, pray do not torment me, Cassandra, with such a question. You alone must know my misery."

"Dear, Jane, I only wish for you to be happy, but I perceive that happiness will be more complicated for you."

Jane now arose and paced with her eyes cast down.

"How I wish I could have fallen in love with an old wealthy earl or duke of some sort, someone who was already too old for children. We would have enough servants to ensure that my domestic duties would be limited to fifteen minutes each day of bossing everyone about. And, certainly, he would need to approve of my writing."

"That is not very likely to happen, is it?"

"Madam Lefroy has been hinting recently that Mr. Lovelace Bigg-Wither may be just that sort of gentleman. But, I cannot conceive of it."

She looked to Cassandra for her reaction.

"The father of my best friends? How unseemly. And, eight children into the bargain. Most importantly, a marriage without love cannot be a happy one, surely. I fear I am doomed to wait for Tom. Or to be a governess, instead of which I would rather die."

"Ah, there you are, Cassandra," said Mr. Austen, entering the dining room, which he did rarely when he knew Jane to be writing. Mrs. Austen followed him, looking ashen. "I have news of a very serious nature, my dear. I have here a letter from Lord Craven, written in February from Santo Domingo. He says that Tom Fowle served him with admirable distinction, and exclaims repeatedly what a gentleman Tom was, and how devoted. He is deeply sorry, my dear. For Tom contracted Yellow Fever this past February. And he is now with his creator. I am so very sorry to bring you this news, my dear."

"Oh, no, it cannot be! No, no, surely you are mistaken, Papa. Say it is not so. Where is the letter? There must be a mistake. He cannot be gone! My own dear Tom!"

She read the letter hastily, and then sank back into her chair in horror. "Oh, how shall I bear it? How shall I live? Why, why, did I let him go?"

"We tried to warn you against him taking such a perilous journey, my dear," offered Mrs. Austen. "And now all is lost. I knew it! I knew this would be the consequence of such a dangerous journey."

Mr. Austen thereupon asked Mrs. Austen to bring a cold cloth for Cassandra's forehead.

"This was no one's fault, Cassandra, and no one could have foreseen it. You are faultless, my dear. We will try to bear it together. We and the Fowles, do not forget their grief, must now accept this blow as best we can. We can never fully understand God's will, I fear, but we can try, with time and with forbearance."

Jane was as stunned as Cassandra, with a hundred disorganized thoughts now swirling in her head. She sank down into her chair and doubled over, letting her tears flow into her lap, sobbing and heaving with unbearable grief. All of the waiting.

All, all was lost.

"I know your strength, Cassandra," consoled Mr. Austen, holding her hand. "I have seen your fortitude. You shall recover, with patience and with faith."

But Cassandra was already far away, beyond consolation, beyond death, reaching for the spirit that was Tom: his smile, his devotion, his love of all that was good. She rose slowly, walked up the stairs to her bed chamber, and closed the door behind her. Jane thought to follow her, but Mr. Austen convinced her that her own condition was not likely to benefit Cassandra's. Cassandra would emerge when she was ready.

"Oh, Papa, this is inconceivable. What does Lord Craven say?" asked Jane.

"He says that Tom was a true and faithful servant to all who knew him. His illness was mercifully short, and he was buried at sea. He says he has also written to the Fowles of the news, and that he will write again tomorrow when he hopes to have gathered his wits about him. He is broken-hearted, poor soul."

"So are we all, I daresay," said Mrs. Austen. "What is to become of us? Who will provide for Cassandra? Or for you, Jane, for that matter?"

Chapter 16

Despite every effort on the part of the Austens, Cassandra was entirely unable to leave her bed chamber during the remaining month of April and most of May. She could not conceive how life could continue around her; how she could still be alive. Time itself seemed to have changed. Her thoughts were slow and heavy, her responses were sluggish, and she wept at it all. During the days, she wept looking out upon the spring garden, and in the evenings, she wept through her father's prayers at her bedside.

Jane brought Cassandra her meals, and read to her from her new manuscript, *First Impressions*, which she wrote with as much humor and foolishness as she could contrive. Mrs. Bennett, the heroine's mother, was an exaggeration of her own mother, of such uncertain temper and fancies over her health as to at last make Cassandra smile as she wept. That was as good a beginning as was possible.

Over the course of these first weeks, Jane began feeling a new purpose. She would help Cassandra recover her life and happiness. Until now, Jane's writing had been thought, by her mother at least, to be self-indulgent, a way to avoid domestic chores and amuse only herself. But now Jane perceived a wider power in it, a power to restore the spirit. She, herself, also became less distressed by waiting for Tom Lefroy, for

Cassandra's circumstances far overshadowed her own. She must now be the stronger and more temperate of the two. The balance had shifted, with Jane giving daily encouragement to Cassandra.

As Cassandra rested the better part of every day, Jane found diversion in walking to Ashe Rectory to talk and laugh with Madam Lefroy. They were both careful not to speak of Tom Lefroy, however. Madam Lefroy, for her part, did not wish for Jane to consider her as primarily a connection to Tom, particularly as Tom had provided no communication regarding Jane in almost a year. And Jane, although she could not help thinking of Tom whenever she visited Madam Lefroy, was afraid of pushing her away by mentioning him. Surely Madam Lefroy would speak if there was anything to say on the subject. Although their visits were always warm and diverting, Jane, nevertheless could not help feel a slight ache upon leaving the rectory, for Tom was forever missing.

Much as she loved Madam Lefroy, Jane's happiest moments were in the company of the Bigg sisters. Catherine was her particular friend, not only because she was the same age, but also because her temperament was closest to Jane's.

"One disadvantage of getting older, aside from losing one's looks, such as they are, is watching one's parents age," said Catherine one day as they walked on the grounds of Manydown. "I had not perceived it before, but now that my father's youngest child is no longer really a child —

Mary-Ann is fourteen, you know — his manner has lost a certain liveliness. It pains me to observe it."

"I wonder he has not remarried. Does he speak of it to you?" asked Jane.

"He considered it a few years ago, I believe, but he did not succeed. The woman was a widow with four children of her own, and I do not suppose she could fathom having eight more of his."

"Was there much affection on his part?"

"Yes, I believe there was, although it is difficult to know that of a parent. He did not speak much of her afterwards. He is still a very handsome gentleman, do you not think?"

"Oh, yes. He must be considered a fine prospect, still," said Jane. "He certainly is to Madam Lefroy, whom I believe still has hopes of his falling violently in love with me, and setting me up for life."

"Oh, that would never do!" laughed Catherine. "You, my stepmother? La, never! My father must seek out a woman past childbearing, to be sure. If he would only visit London or Bath during the season, he would meet with a great many accomplished women," said Catherine. "But he will not. He finds it all unseemly and excessive."

"I quite share his view. It must seem very like two opposing parades, with women in one, and men in the other, passing each other until a suitable match is found. Quite demoralizing, really. I have no taste for it, myself."

"But unless my father is more active in

seeking out someone, I fear he risks being passively found, without much thought. There is a certain woman now whom I believe has set her eyes upon him. Her name is Augusta Croft, of Northern England. Have you heard of her?"

"No, I have not had the pleasure."

"Oh, then, pray, stay with us for tea today. Miss Croft is to come. I wish to know your opinion of her. I cannot quite make her out. She is excessively attentive to my father and to all of us. But there is something about her, I cannot say what, that gives me unease. Lizzy mentioned it to me, as well, when Miss Croft came for tea last week. She seems a bit desperate."

"I thank you, yes, I should be pleased to stay for tea, if you wish it."

"Of course, dear Heathcote will be here, too. He has become quite one of the family, although Lizzy slights him still. She is still determined to find a wealthy husband."

Chapter 17

"What an enchanting room!" cried Mr. Collier, Reverend Heathcote's curate, who was invited to tea along with Heathcote. "How you must anticipate every meal with relish for the honor of gazing upon this wallpaper! It is elegance itself, is it not, Heathcote? And the candles — twelve of them, to be sure. Only observe how the cream of the candles is a perfect match to the ground of the paper. Uncanny, I call it. Do you consult a specialist in the field, sir, when choosing the patterns and colors for Manydown? For, many of your peers do, I believe."

"No, no, I have never thought of it," said Mr. Bigg-Wither. "The late Mrs. Bigg-Wither chose all the furnishings here, and the servants find candles where they may. I am, myself, a poor judge of such matters."

"A happy accident, then, is it not?" asked Mr. Collier of Alethea, the youngest of the three sisters. "And the brocade of these chairs is quite good. Quite good, indeed. I flatter myself to be somewhat of a connoisseur of fine textiles. It is one of my little hobbies."

"Oh, and how came that to be, sir?" asked Alethea, with a quick look at Catherine.

"Why, I have made a study of the pews in every parish I have had the good fortune to visit, my dear. While satin velvet will always remain the standard-bearer of fine pew seating, the nap of that textile does, alas, have a tendency to show wear over time. But brocade! Why, it wears well for a dozen years or more. Its age can really only be determined by close examination of the fibers, and whether it gives off a musty sort of odor, as it often does after ten years or so, I have observed."

"Jane, would you do me the honor of being seated next to me?" asked Mr. Bigg-Wither. "I have not heard of Cassandra's health recently. How does she? Dare we hope for her health to be restored?"

"I thank you, sir. You are very good. Cassandra improves daily, I believe. She will certainly remain in mourning until February, but we have every hope of her restoration."

"By the bye, my dear, textile restoration is another of my little hobbies," whispered Collier to Alethea, who was studying her food. He was keenly aware that a suitor to a woman of fortune must distinguish himself in some notable accomplishment.

"What is that you say, Mr. Collier?" asked Miss Croft. "I am excessively interested in home furnishings, you know. Indeed, I had noticed the brocade, as well, and was about to remark upon it."

"How very s-s-singular to have such a c-c-convergence of home furnishing experts in our own h-h-humble abode," joined Harris. "Perhaps, Miss Croft, you could be p-p-persuaded to provide my father with your ideas of a c-c-complete renovation of our f-f-furnishings."

"With pleasure, I assure you," cooed Miss Croft at Mr. Bigg-Wither. "Nothing could please me more."

"I can see no occasion for that," said Mr. Bigg-Wither. "I have been well satisfied with every thing all these years."

"You will pardon my saying so, sir, but as I mentioned, the brocade may well..." reminded Collier.

"Say no more, sir. Yes, yes, madam. By all means. Do as you wish," said Mr. Bigg-Wither.

Having made this satisfactory inroad, Miss Croft ventured to cast her net a little farther.

"Miss Austen, I would be very much pleased for us to become better acquainted. You live in the neighborhood, I believe?" asked Miss Croft.

"Yes, not two miles away. Catherine and Lizzy and Alethea are my dearest friends. I count myself most fortunate," answered Jane.

"And your father? Is he a gentleman, as well?"

"Yes. He is the minister of both the Steventon and Dean parishes. May I inquire, madam, do you live in London? Or in Bath, perhaps?"

"Why, no, although I dearly love them both. So much activity, you know, and all manner of gaiety. No, my family is from Scarborough, quite north of here. It is not nearly so bustling, of course. But it is the best place I know since all my early memories reside there," said Miss Croft.

"Are you quite sure, Miss Croft? My

recollection is that your family resides in Middlesbrough," said Mr. Bigg-Wither. "Perhaps my memory is faulty, however."

"Oh, dear, I believe I misspoke! Silly of me, really. I have some relations in Scarborough whom I spent a great deal of time with as a girl. That is what I meant. Wonderful memories."

"Ah, I do love S-S-Scarborough, myself," said Harris. "Tell me, is the famous Black C-C-Crow tavern still on the green in the center of t-t-town?"

"Certainly it is. And widely known for its amiable hospitality, too," said Miss Croft.

"I am very glad to hear of this, Miss Croft," said Heathcote, "as I plan to travel north in the next few weeks to visit my own family. I shall look in at the Black Crow if Scarborough is along my path. My family is in Glasgow."

"We shall miss your company, Heathcote, shall we not, Lizzy? Pray, how long will you be out of the country?" asked Mr. Bigg-Wither.

"My plans are not entirely settled, but I may be absent for two or three weeks together. But do not fear, for I have every confidence that Mr. Collier will minister to the congregation extremely well in my absence. If you wish it, I would be delighted to send a letter or two," said Heathcote.

"Of course we wish it, do we not, girls?"

Shortly after tea, Harris sought out Heathcote, and found him alone in the library.

"I say, sir. May I s-s-speak to you on a matter of some d-d-delicacy?" asked Harris.

"By all means, my boy. I hope you never doubt my interest in anything you wish to discuss. Is it of a devotional nature?"

"Hardly, sir. It is only that there is no Black C-C-Crow tavern in Scarborough. At least, that I know of. I m-m-made it up, you see."

"What? What could you mean by it?"

"Only that I have my s-s-suspicions about Miss Croft, and meant to put her to the t-t-test. She took the bait and swallowed it, as you observed. I wish to protect my father from any sort of m-m-mischief, but I am unsure of what to do with the information. What is your opinion? Would he resent my m-mentioning it?"

"Oh dear," said Heathcote. "Oh dear. Let me consider. Miss Croft could well claim that she misheard the name, or became confused again, if your father were to point out the error. But no, he would not wish to cause her discomfort. His manners would not permit it. Say nothing of it to him at present, and let me take the burden. I shall be sure to travel through Scarborough, after all, and inquire after the Crofts. Be assured, my boy, that you did right in bringing this matter to me, and that I shall see it through. I love your father too dearly to see him ill used, I assure you."

Chapter 18

Heathcote did then alter his plans to take a longer route to Glasgow in July. Upon entering the town of Scarborough, he inquired after the Black Crow tavern, and was told by a resident that no such establishment had ever existed there.

"It is my error, no doubt. I thank you, sir," said Heathcote.

"I could recommend to you the Lion and Shield, sir, if you would be so pleased. My own sister's family have been the proprietors of that establishment these fifty years. There is no better inn to be had, I assure you," said the man.

"I may travel on to Middlesbrough today, after all. It is still early in the day. But tell me, sir, do you know anything of the Croft family here? An acquaintance has mentioned that she spent some part of her youth with that family."

"Alas, it appears that I have but empty news for you again, sir. I have lived my entire life in Scarborough without that name being mentioned. You are certain of the name?"

"Not entirely certain, now that I reconsider. I may have been mistaken there, as well. I do apologize for taking up your time. You have been most helpful."

"I would not call it helpful, sir, but I am happy to be of service."

Heathcote arrived in Middlesbrough on that

afternoon's coach. Upon inquiring after the family of Croft in that even smaller town, he became convinced that no such family had ever resided there, either.

That's curious, thought he. There can now be no doubt that Miss Croft, if that is indeed her name, is an impostor. How shall I inform Mr. Bigg-Wither in such a manner as to protect him from her wrath at being discovered?

A few weeks later, the Bigg sisters visited Steventon Rectory, laughing and gossiping with Jane along the lanes, where they would not be overheard by anyone of the family. Alethea and Catherine were almost walking backwards on the gravel in front of Jane and Lizzy as they spoke.

"I declare I do not care a fig for any of the men I have met," laughed Alethea. "I except your excellent brothers, Jane. But you know my meaning. They are forever going on one adventure or another, leaving us quite forgotten. It is ill use, I say, and I will not have it."

"What *will* you have?" asked Jane. "What do you propose? If you do not marry, will you not, then, be entirely forgotten?"

"I wish to live a life of my own, that is all, surrounded by my family and friends and horses and dogs. Someone must care for my father, you know, and I am happy to do it," said Alethea.

"And when your father is gone?" asked Jane. "What then?"

"Why, I shall take care of Harris until he

marries. I have no wish to reside anywhere except Manydown. What about you? Do you wish absolutely to leave Steventon?" asked Alethea.

"No, but I have no fortune of my own, so it is quite another matter. *I* shall be the forgotten one, I fear," smiled Jane.

"Then come to Manydown! You shall always have a home there," said Alethea. "We shall adopt you!"

"Yes, yes. I am quite in favor of that," said Lizzy. "And if I am to marry a gentleman of fortune, you shall be very welcome with us. I will insist upon it," said Lizzy.

"You are all goodness. I could not wish for better friends. But,if I could not marry a gentleman whom I could truly admire and esteem, I would conspire to have fame and a fortune of my own," laughed Jane. "But Lizzy, you already have the conditions for happiness. You simply will not own them. It is most provoking for your friends to witness. You have a fortune, Heathcote is a man much admired and esteemed, and he is not likely to ever forget you. Can you doubt it?"

"No, I cannot. His letters from Glasgow to my father have mentioned me several times. I suppose I am attached to the fantasies of my childhood — to marry someone of my father's stature."

"Everyone except you believes him to be already of your father's stature," said Jane.

"I, for one, miss seeing him here," said

Catherine. "If his heart were unattached, he would be my own object, I declare. I have never met with such devotion as he shows to you, Lizzy. You cannot take him for granted forever, however. He may eventually despair of ever winning your affections, and may at last turn to me."

"La! How can you say so? To have such a sister! Is it not shameful, Jane?" asked Lizzy.

"It would be an honor to have such a sister. I know it, for I already have such a one," said Jane.

Chapter 19

Never had there been such an avid lover of home furnishings as Miss Augusta Croft was. There could be no peace at Manydown, such was the flurry of activities and considerations in the pursuit of refinement and taste. In fact, some of the Bigg-Wither household became determined never to care for a scrap of taste again, if such a thing could be identified and tackled to the ground.

This did not include Mr. Bigg-Wither, however, who progressed from initial alarm to complaisance within the course of only a few weeks. It was good to have a woman again at Manydown. Her temper was only sharp when she was not obeyed, and she kept the servants in line with efficacy. And, her opinions were frequent enough that Mr. Bigg-Wither was seldom required for his. All had been thought through, and the household and servants were completely under her control, including the horses and dogs. In fact, life had become so easy for Mr. Bigg-Wither that he began to consider the benefits of making Miss Croft an offer of marriage. For where could her equal be found? She was a marvel in addition to being handsome. And, she had made little secret of her attachment to Manydown. She loved it quite as her own, she declared.

Heathcote, in the meanwhile, was enjoying the beauties of the countryside surrounding his family's home in Glasgow. He exercised his favorite horse in the green groves and woods almost daily, and was frequently invited to the hunting parties of the neighbors, some of whom he had known since childhood.

One morning before a hunt he was introduced to a Mr. Campbell, the friend of a neighbor. Upon further acquaintance, he learned that Mr. Campbell's wife had left him some six months prior. To this distress was added the circumstance of her also having left their three-year-old mentally deficient son, declaring that she would no longer bear that burden, and would seek her fortune elsewhere. Mr. Campbell feared she was not likely to return, although he wished it for the sake of their son. She had not been discovered in London or in Bath, although she could be easily identified by a crescent-shaped birthmark on her right hand. However, she disliked the birthmark, and usually wore gloves.

After several weeks of relaxation in the countryside, Heathcote returned to his Basingstoke rectory late on a Saturday evening. The next morning, he greeted his parishioners with his usual welcoming warmth at the large front door, including the Bigg-Wither family, accompanied by Miss Croft. When the time came for Holy Communion, when the silver chalice of wine was offered to Miss Croft, Heathcote bent low to her ear and whispered, "Madam, surely there can be no barrier between you and your God." Then he waited while motioning with his eyes to her right glove. Taken unawares, Miss Croft hastily removed it to avoid offense.

Upon leaving the church after the service, Mr. Bigg-Wither inquired at the door whether he and Miss Croft might have the pleasure of Heathcote's company to Manydown for dinner, for the two of them had a matter to discuss with him in private.

After shutting the church for the day, and at last settling into the carriage, Heathcote began the conversation with, "Madam, you have a remarkable attachment to the Bigg-Wither home and family, I believe."

"Indeed I do, sir. Manydown is dearer to me than any other place I have known. And the family, yes, I do love them, I confess."

"It must be a prodigious inconvenience to your own family, surely," replied Heathcote.

"What can you mean by such a suggestion, sir? You are quite mistaken. I have no living family to be inconvenienced."

"You have none in Scarborough nor in Middlesbrough, that much is certain. I can personally attest to it, for I have inquired there myself. No Crofts have ever resided in either town. Nor has there been a Black Crow Inn. Come, come, what can you mean by these deceptions, madam, and what other deceptions are we to expect?"

"Oh, how can you speak in such a manner? I call it disgraceful in a clergyman to behave so! If I have made a wee error in recalling a town or two, you cannot fairly paint me as a villainess. Why do you not come to my aid, Mr. Bigg-Wither, as any gentleman would?" said she, when he simply looked aghast.

"Perhaps it is precisely because he *is* a gentleman. I could have wished Mr. Bigg-Wither to accompany me to Glasgow, where I met by chance a gentleman by the name of George Campbell. Have you been to Glasgow, madam? Do you know of him? He has a young son who was born mentally deficient. To add to his misfortunes, Mr. Campbell's wife left him some six months ago, declaring that she would not be burdened with such a child, and that she would seek a better life elsewhere. She had, he said, a curious birthmark in the pattern of a crescent moon on her right hand, which she hid by always wearing gloves. That must be the current fashion, madam, for one cannot avoid noticing that such is your habit, as well."

At last regaining his voice, Mr. Bigg-Wither said, "Come, Augusta, let us put an end to the matter. Let there be no suspicion. My dear, I entreat you to remove your gloves."

"Mr. Bigg-Wither, I must protest this attempt at intimidation. I consider it shocking that I should be abused in this manner. I have an unsightly rash on my hands, that is all. That is why I never reveal them in public, and I refuse to do so now. There is an end to the matter."

She turned her back to the gentlemen.

"Madam, I saw the birthmark on your hand during Holy Communion. Can you deny it?"

There was no answer.

"I shall insist upon you removing your right glove, madam," said Heathcote, "or you shall be turned out upon this road."

Slowly, and in anger, she finally did so. "Do you suppose that I am the only creature with a birthmark? I have seen several such birthmarks, myself. I am especially attentive to such things since I have one, but *you* may not have particular reason to notice them."

Heathcote then pulled a scrap of paper from his pocket. It opened to reveal the name "Mrs. Mary Campbell," and a sketch of a right hand with a crescent moon of exactly the same shape, size, and location of that of Miss Croft.

"Mrs. Campbell! How we have been deceived!" cried Mr. Bigg-Wither. "This is too shocking to be borne!" He face was in blustery shades of red.

Heathcote then ordered the driver to return to Basingstoke, during which, Mrs. Campbell simpered and begged Mr. Bigg-Wither to consider their mutual attachment as well as the unfinished state of Manydown's furnishings. But he would not be moved.

Once in Basingstoke, Heathcote purchased a carriage ticket to Glasgow for Mrs. Campbell, and assured her that her belongings would be forwarded promptly to Mr. George Campbell.

While handing her onto the carriage, Heathcote whispered to her, "Do not doubt, madam, that you have the means of being forgiven by your God, if you would only truly repent. It is within your own power."

Chapter 20

"I cannot express enough, my dear, how gratifying it is to see you this morning. You are returned to us at last," said Mr. Austen. "How we have missed your countenance."

"Say no more, Papa, or I shall weep again," said Cassandra. "I scarcely know where I have been or where I am going. But I am here, and I shall try." Although her tears started welling up, she was able this time to hold them in check.

"Well, I shall hazard a guess," said Jane. "You have had quite enough of my ill-prepared breakfasts, and hoped for better by coming down to see what else Cook can provide."

"Oh, no, Jane. You have kept me alive. Truly. You have made me laugh every day. I can never repay you."

"You will have done when you are strong enough to take some exercise with me in the garden. Only a half-hour will do. We've had the most glorious July. Everything's in bloom and waiting for you," said Jane.

"And my dear, we have so many berries this year that we have enough to give away fresh. When you feel equal to it, you may take some to Manydown," added Mrs. Austen.

"Yes, yes, everyone inquires after you. It will be quite a treat for you to turn up," said Jane.

And, so it was. A few days later, all the Biggs

and Bigg-Withers came out to see the Austen carriage pull up, and to see Cassandra and Jane emerge with berries.

Lizzy took Cassandra's hands, and twirled her around, so glad was she to see her friend again. It had been over two months of worrying and waiting.

"Pray, do not make such a fuss, Lizzy. I am the same old Cassandra, I assure you. And thank you for all your kind inquiries. How very fortunate I am to have such friends. I cannot think what I have done to deserve it."

"Come, come, my dears, Cook has prepared an excellent lunch in Cassandra's honor," beamed Mr. Bigg-Wither. "Let us not keep her waiting."

"Oh, sir, this hall is changed," said Cassandra. "I barely recognize it. Look, Jane, new sconces, new little benches. Very fashionable, is it not? I like it all very much. Was this your doing, Lizzy?"

"You must know, Cassandra, that I have been much deceived in Miss Croft," said Mr. Bigg-Wither, somberly, over lunch. "It has been very shocking for us all. Had it not been for the quick perception and action of Mr. Heathcote to discover her infamous past, why, I should be the unfortunate husband of a bigamist. A bigamist! I shudder to think of it. The legal entanglements, our reputation in society. What if there had been a child? What a scandal! I am mortified, still."

"Oh, dear sir, all who know you cannot

doubt your innocence in the matter. To be used so outrageously. And Mr. Heathcote discovered her past, you say?" asked Cassandra, looking at Lizzy.

"A hero, I call him. We owe him more than I can express. I consulted my solicitor last week, and have made provisions for Heathcote to receive a goodly portion of land in Manydown Park. He deserves no less for his service to this family. I shall help him build a manor, if he chooses, or a lodge, if he wishes to use it for hunting. There are many tenants on that land, so I expect his living will be handsome enough for a large family," said Mr. Bigg-Wither with a smile. "If he so chooses."

Not a few eyes shifted to Lizzy, who looked about, bewildered.

"If he so chooses," repeated Mr. Bigg-Wither.

"I call that very generous, sir," said Cassandra. "It is perhaps premature to know what Mr. Heathcote may choose."

"But, we may s-s-surmise that good Mr. Collier stands at the ready to assist with the f-f-furnishings, as well as with his clerical duties," said Harris. "Mr. Heathcote is, indeed, a f-f-fortunate man."

Jane was fortunate, as well, for she stored away the incident to be brought forth again in *First Impressions*: a gentleman pursuing and discovering a villain, saving the reputation of a family whose daughter he loves. Yes, that would do very well.

Chapter 21

The trip to Manydown was Cassandra's first real exertion these last two months. The joy of reuniting with her friends overcame her fatigue for the afternoon, but she was again exhausted in the evening, and retired early.

The next day, she asked Jane, "Do you suppose Harris resented the gift of land to Mr. Heathcote? Harris seems so odd, you know. I cannot determine whether he would admire such a grand gesture by Mr. Bigg-Wither since it will diminish his own expectations."

"Oh, no, I should think not. Harris's reputation is spared, as well, you know. Such a scandal would have affected them all. Heathcote is the sort of man, I believe, who would protect her whether she ever deigns to accept him or not. That is my idea of a gentleman. And of love. Such disinterested devotion is not often to be met with."

Jane turned away. She had been determined not to speak of anything that could remind her of Tom Lefroy. But now, as the words came from her own mouth, the pain of being abandoned by her own Tom for a year and a half rose to the surface again. She could not call Tom's behavior gentlemanly, nor could she call it love. He had not visited, and no message had been communicated through Madam Lefroy. It was difficult to continue justifying his behavior, to admire less gentlemanly behavior than what she saw in Heathcote, who would never abandon Lizzy in such a manner. And Lizzy had provided no encouragement to Heathcote whatsoever. There was little reason for Jane to continue to hope, and yet she did. No one else had captured her heart so completely, nor was anyone ever likely to do so again. And she was convinced Tom Lefroy loved her. Indeed, many years later, when Tom Lefroy was Lord Chief Justice of Ireland, he admitted that he had loved her. Jane had not been wrong.

"Dear Jane. How strong you have been for me when I know your own heart is aching. I know that it is over for me. I shall never love anyone else, for I shall never stop loving my Tom. That is my destiny. But yours is still before you. Do you not feel that?"

"It is difficult to know what I feel. I am tired of it all, that much I know. I wish I could feel less. My poor head might be spared so many conflicting thoughts, and I could be more at ease.

"It has helped me to be by your side," she continued. "That much I do know. And, it has helped me to write. That is when I am most certain of anything. I can see the lives of the Bennets and Mr. Darcy more clearly than my own."

"I admire Mr. Darcy more and more. He is becoming a hero to me. And as his real nature is discovered, I find less and less to admire in Tom Lefroy. I wish it were not so, but I cannot escape the truth of it much longer. Some day, I suppose, my feelings for Tom will meet the truth in bright daylight and be forever changed. But that has not yet happened. I continue to hope without reason. To love without reason."

"Let us remove reason, then. As for me, I love without hope," said Cassandra. "Even hope can be removed, so that only love remains, without reason and without hope."

"But that is no life, surely. That is not happiness. It may be a sort of contentment, and that may be sufficient for old spinsters, I suppose. But we are in our prime, Cassandra. And I am determined to live actively, like Elizabeth Bennet. She will push forward.

"Oh Cassandra, that reminds me. I have just finished a passage that has diverted me excessively. I cannot read it without laughing, myself. You remember Mr. Collins, of course. Quite ridiculous. I have rewritten his foolish proposal to Elizabeth. Ah, here is the last portion."

"You should take it into further consideration, that despite your manifold attractions, it is by no means certain that another offer of marriage may ever be made you. Your portion is unhappily so small that it will in all likelihood undo the effects of your loveliness and amiable qualifications. As I must therefore conclude that you are not serious in your rejection of me, I shall choose to attribute it to your wish of increasing my love by suspense, according to the usual practice of elegant ladies."

"Jane, you are killing me," laughed Cassandra. "Oh, he is the most odious man alive."

"He is almost alive, is he not?" asked Jane. "A simpering little booby of a man. I could laugh at him all day."

"But, Jane, how do you do it? He comes from your own mind, but you could never say such things. Where does it come from?"

"Why, I am borrowing Mr. Collier. Only imagine that he were to offer a declaration to Alethea. What could he say to make her want to strangle him? That is all. I like him exceedingly. He shall go after Charlotte next, and do it again."

"Oh, Jane. But consider. Who will read it? What will mother think?"

"What care I what she thinks? It is Mr. Collins, not me. He *will* speak."

It was just a few weeks later when Jane's assertion was put to the test. She had now completed *First Impressions,* and brought it out to be read to her parents.

"I do not find Mr. Collins nearly as horrid as you seem to do. I agree with Charlotte," said Mrs. Austen. "There is much to be said for having a comfortable home. Half the world cannot boast so much. What does it matter that her husband is disagreeable, unless she is required to spend every minute of the day with him? Charlotte is twenty and seven. Pray, what are the Lucases to do with her at that age?"

"Mrs. Austen, the material point is that tempers differ," said Mr. Austen. "To many of both sexes, I believe, marriage without love is insupportable. They cannot help it if love does not materialize. They formulate other arrangements and activities in their lives to provide happiness."

"And what of their parents? They would be brought to the poorhouse if every girl were to dither her youth away dreaming of romance."

As this conversation proceeded rather too closely towards circumstances at hand, Jane thought to end the reading for the evening, and attempt another chapter the next day.

"My dear," said Mr. Austen privately to Jane a little later. "You have a gift. Indeed you do. I have not read its equal in perception, exposition, and charm since Richardson. You surpass him in many respects, to my mind. And, the narrative form certainly suits the comprehension of the entire community of characters. You have done well, my dear. I am prodigiously proud of you. Whether this work comes to be published or not, you have here a work of quality that can never be taken away."

"I think of it as my own child, Papa. I am as proud of it as any mother could be. I thank you, sir."

Chapter 22

It was October of 1797 before Cassandra could be said to have regained normalcy after learning of Tom Fowle's death. She could never be the same as before she met him, nor could she be the same as while he was living. But, she had found a stability in thinking and feeling. She found pleasure in domesticity and work again. There were satisfactions in darning a sock properly, in covering a small footstool beautifully, and in seeing to the livestock in the back court. She did all these with thoughts of Tom. He was in everything she saw and felt and did. His love of animals encouraged her to plan for a better roof for the horses and a more comfortable coop for the chickens as the cold weather approached. She knew he would be pleased.

"Well, Cassandra, *First Impressions* has been put away now in my writing box to hibernate," said Jane one afternoon as she came into the garden and sat beside Cassandra on the stone bench. "When it wakes up, it may say something new. Or it may surprise me by changing its mind about everything."

"How can you say so?" asked Cassandra. "Is it not you who makes those decisions? Do you not mean that *you* may change your mind?"

"I may, but it is more likely that the characters, themselves, will. They may stew in each other's company in such a way as to develop new ideas. Miss Anne de Bourgh's health may improve and embolden her to claim Mr. Darcy. Conversely, Mr. Darcy could become ill. Or, Colonel Fitzwilliam could fall violently in love with Lizzy."

"You cannot be in earnest, surely. It is perfect as it is."

"But *they* are not," said Jane. "In any case, I flatter myself that the narrative form has proved less difficult than I feared. I have a mind to dig up *Elinor and Marianne* from the box, and re-write it now as a narrative."

"One does tire of reading so many letters. But will you change it materially? Will either of their personalities be shown to be superior? What think you now?"

"Elinor is more of how you behaved with your Tom, and Marianne is more of how I behaved with my Tom. You have more sense, and I have more sensibility. But, for all her faults, Marianne cannot be diminished or discarded," said Jane. "You wish to make me a philosopher, Cassandra, which is something I shall never be. I change my mind too often. It is only on that point that I never change."

Jane and Cassandra were now summoned to the parlor, for their Aunt Leigh-Perrot, whose husband James was Mrs. Austen's brother, had come to visit.

"My dears, here is a brilliant plan! What do you think? Aunt Leigh-Perrot has invited the three of us to join her in Bath for November. What an honor, and so generous, is it not, girls? What say you to that? Is this not kindness in your aunt? Oh, the social life, the shops, the assemblies. All the most fashionable families and eligible gentlemen, you know."

"Oh, you are too kind, Aunt," said Jane. "I am overcome. I know not how to respond. Bath! I need time to consider."

This evasion provided just the few seconds Cassandra needed to determine how to decline as politely as possible. Neither Jane nor Cassandra could tolerate a proximity to Aunt Leigh-Perrot for very long.

"I thank you with all my heart, Aunt. It is a most generous offer. But, as you see, I am in mourning for my late fiance, Mr. Fowle. I am therefore unable to accept your kind offer this season. My feelings in every respect forbid it." Cassandra had been wearing black for mourning every day since May, and would continue until February, as proper behavior dictated.

Cassandra glanced over at Jane, whose eyes had widened considerably. Jane did not want to go, either.

Cassandra then hastened to add, "I credit my sister for caring for me every day. Indeed, I know not how I should have recovered without her kind assistance."

She quickened her pace again. "She is still my daily comfort. I cannot conceive of losing her so soon, and for so long. Pray, do not remove her. I am not entirely well."

"Oh, pish, Cassandra. You are as well as you choose to be. And if you are not, I shall certainly care for you as I have all my life. But would Bath be quite proper, sister, since she is in mourning?" asked Mrs. Austen.

"I daresay, Cassandra's enjoyment and activity might well be curtailed by her present condition. There is something in that," acknowledged Mrs. Leigh-Perrot. "But, she may benefit from the bustle and activity and change of scene without attending assemblies and parties and the theater. Yes, I think it will improve your spirits prodigiously, Cassandra. Just the thing. And Jane will be there, too, you know."

"Jane," said Mrs. Austen. "What a chance for you, now. I trust you have outgrown your unseemly flirtations of the past, and will do what is necessary to secure your future."

"Pray, what is your age, Jane?" asked Mrs. Leigh-Perrot.

"I am just twenty-one, Aunt."

"She will be twenty-two next month. So, you see, how urgent…oh, I do not mean urgent. But how very welcome such an opportunity to enjoy herself and meet fashionable families must be. And gentlemen. She is quite tired of everyone here."

There was now no assistance to be hoped for, short of an act of God.

"I would be delighted, then. I shall look forward very much to accompany you. One hears a great deal about Bath," said Jane.

To be sure, one heard that London was the place of vice and dissipation, that Bath was the place of health spas and high society, and that those attractions may well have some connection. Yes, perhaps the journey would not be so very bad, and could offer some amusement.

On the other hand, few things in Jane's estimation could be less amusing than the company of Aunt Leigh-Perrot. The prospect of a month without respite of Mrs. Austen together with Aunt Leigh-Perrot was daunting. Only the consolation of Cassandra accompanying them could offer any comfort.

In the several weeks before the journey, in part to distract herself from the inevitable misery, Jane did resurrect the *Elinor and Marianne* manuscript, and read it again afresh. The experience was an odd mixture of familiarity and surprise. She had, of course, written every word, but had in part forgotten what she wrote, even though she felt as though she carried the characters around with her. Page after page surprised her, and made her laugh again, just as she had when the ideas first came to her.

Chapter 23

Bath's social season had begun in October, filling up all the available houses and rooms with aspirants. But, because the Leigh-Perrots resided in Bath during every winter season, they could not be said to aspire to anything beyond being continually seen and admired, which they were. Rather, being rich conferred to them certain entitlements, not the least of which was the right of condescension. The most satisfying of these, of course, was condescension towards the lesser branches of their family.

It was in this spirit that the Leigh-Perrots welcomed the Austen women into their home. Mrs. Austen, a woman of elusive health complaints, would benefit from the mineral waters, Cassandra would benefit from a change of scene and society after her shocking loss, and Jane was in need of a husband before she surpassed a respectable age for marriage.

"You have the benefit of separate bedrooms in our house, my dears," said Aunt Leigh-Perrot. "You may have the privacy here that is seldom to be found at the rectory, I suppose."

"Aunt, you are too good," said Jane. "Your home is vast enough for anyone's privacy. But, as it happens, Cassandra and I prefer using the same bed chamber. With all the privacy to be had here during the day, we would miss each other's company altogether otherwise."

"Cassandra, can this be your preference, too?" asked Aunt Leigh-Perrot. "As you are in mourning, you may wish to spend more of your time in reflection, I suppose."

"Quite the contrary, I assure you, Aunt," said Cassandra. "Solitary reflection has nearly cost me the balance of my mind. I find talking over the day with Jane in the morning and in the evening to be quite a benefit."

"In addition to prayers, I should think," added Mrs. Leigh-Perrot.

"Certainly. Without fail," assured Cassandra.

The days were pleasant enough, although it was a particularly rainy month. Walking excursions were organized on fine days to the various interesting places. They drank the healthy water at the Pump Room, and Aunt Leigh-Perrot purchased all three of them new silk bonnets of the latest fashion in a shop where she was well known. She did, however, somewhat regret the purchases later in the evening, lamenting, unaccountably, over Mr. Leigh-Perrot's poor finances. Cassandra, of course, would not wear hers until she was out of mourning. Indeed, Cassandra stayed at home with Mr. Leigh-Perrot most evenings while Mrs. Austen, Jane, and Aunt Leigh-Perrot attended assemblies and the theater.

"I would like to introduce you to a gentleman very well worth your knowing," said Aunt Leigh-Perrot one evening to Mrs. Austen and

Jane at the assembly rooms. "Mr. William Thackney, may I introduce to you my sister, Mrs. George Austen, and to my niece, Miss Jane Austen?"

"With pleasure, I assure you. How do you do? I have heard much of your visit from your aunt."

"Indeed? Are we infamous already?" laughed Jane. "And with so little effort. What could we have done, pray, to merit such notice?"

"Why, nothing in particular, to be sure. I meant only that your arrival has been well-anticipated by your aunt and uncle. I have the honor, you see, of being the Leigh-Perrot's banker. As such, we speak frequently on friendly as well as on financial matters."

"Oh, Mr. Banker!" cried Mrs. Austen. "I mean Mr. Hackney. I beg your pardon. You do us honor, I am sure. A banker! Why, that is vastly interesting. So much money, you know."

"Quite so. Yes. The name, again, is Thackney, madam. But, what particularly interests me is in the planning of estates, and so forth. One must know the law, as well."

This particular topic created a small pause, providing an opening for Mr. Thackney to ask whether he might have the honor of the next two dances with Miss Austen, to which she happily consented.

Many a young lady has been gratified by how a very good dance partner constituted the highlight of an assembly, regardless of who he was.

Lisa L. Jorgensen

And so it was on this occasion. In addition, Jane was desperate to escape the supervision of her mother and aunt, who had hovered over her for days. There was no privacy to be had anywhere. Dancing with the elegant Mr. Thackney was exactly what she wanted.

"Do you come to the assemblies often, Mr. Thackney?" Jane asked.

"No, no, very seldom."

Here he paused.

"I may say that when I was younger, I did come here with some regularity. But that is some years past."

"That is a pity, sir. How fortunate, then, that you should be here this evening. To what do we owe the honor?"

"Why, Mrs. Leigh-Perrot mentioned that..."

"Ah, it was as a courtesy to my aunt."

"I should say rather that it was as a courtesy to you, Miss Austen. She wished for you to enjoy dancing, and knew that I had enjoyed it myself some years ago."

"She was, perhaps, concerned that I might not be asked to dance?" asked Jane.

"I cannot say. But she meant it kindly, I can assure you."

"And do you expect a bonus envelope for your attentions, sir, or has that already been seen to?"

Jane had now stepped away from the dance altogether.

"Why, I cannot say, Miss Austen. The Leigh-Perrots have always rewarded me well, to be sure."

This was too humiliating! Her own family had so little faith in her ability to secure a partner that they had paid someone to show interest. She would have none of it.

"Mamma, I wish to return home directly. I fear I have over-exerted myself."

"Why then sit down for a little, my dear, and rest. There are refreshments and punch to be had, you know. Will they not be welcome?" asked Mrs. Austen. "There are so many elegant gentlemen here, are there not? Is that not an inducement to stay a little longer?"

"Not in the least. I wish to return home, if you please. I am quite sick of elegant gentlemen."

Upon returning, she found Cassandra already asleep, but Jane's sniffling work her up.

"Our aunt paid someone to ask me to dance, Cassandra. I cannot bear it. Am I such a monstrous creature that no one will dance with me of their own volition?"

"Oh, Jane. No, no. Perhaps she meant to display your dancing so others would wish to be next. You are an excellent dancer, after all."

"I would not wish that to be my primary attraction. I will take no pleasure in it, if that is the case.

"Cassandra, I have been thinking of something on the way home. Do you suppose that Madam Lefroy also paid Tom Lefroy to be interested in me? And that he never intended to return?"

"Jane, you must stop now. You have taken this too much to heart. I am very sorry that our aunt asked the gentleman to pay you attention, for I am sure, left on your own, you would have danced many dances. You do at Steventon and Basingstoke, after all."

"But everyone knows me there, and perhaps feels a neighborly obligation."

"Really, Jane, you know that to be false. You have many admirers. I'm afraid this evening has stirred too many reminders of Tom for you."

"Well, this evening would not have occurred had Tom been gentleman enough to return. I have become a case for charity. Oh, had we never come here. The weather is abominable, and I miss our garden, our woods, our walks. I also miss Mr. Darcy and Elizabeth Bennet."

Someone else had been thinking of them, as well. For when the Austen women had removed to Bath, Mr. Austen had taken it upon himself to write to Mr. Thomas Cadell, a London publisher, to see if *First Impressions* could be published, so convinced was he of its merit. He wrote that it was a work in three volumes of about the same length as Fanny Burney's popular *Evelina*. The envelope was returned, however, with "Declined by Return of Post" stamped across the top of it. It had not even been opened. Mr. Cadell had not seen fit to consider a letter from a stranger. At least, consoled Mr.

Austen to himself, it could be no reflection on the manuscript's worth. But that was an empty consolation.

Mr. Austen thereupon gave the envelope to the fire, and determined never to tell Jane of it. Perhaps another opportunity would present itself in the future.

Chapter 24

December in Steventon was as fair as
November in Bath had been rainy. Both Jane and
Cassandra were very happy to return, and even
more so when they next visited Manydown. For a
miracle had taken place in their absence. Lizzy had
at last accepted Heathcote.

"No, no," said Lizzy. "While it can truthfully
be said that he was persistent, it cannot be said that
I simply gave way, that I grew too tired to object.
No, there was more.

"I had always admired him, you know, as a
protege of my father, for his understanding, his
generosity of spirit, and his attention to me, of
course. What I came to feel, however, began with
his pursuit and exposure of Miss Croft. That spoke
of devotion not only to me, but to our family, our
reputation, and our inheritance. I wept when his full
goodness made itself plain to me. How could there
be such another man?"

"How fortunate you are, Lizzy. I wish you
joy a thousand times over," said Cassandra. Her
genuinely felt good wishes did not entirely mask
her own pain in this event, much as she made the
attempt. Jane sought quickly to divert her from
thoughts of her loss.

"And your father, what of his feelings upon
this offer?" asked Jane.

"Oh, wait until you hear. One of my

misgivings had been that perhaps Heathcote could not measure up to my father. When I confessed this to my father, he took Heathcote's part completely. He said that he, in fact, admired Heathcote above all others, that I had it completely wrong. My father said that when he was in doubt upon a decision, he always considered what Heathcote would do in his place. Heathcote, in his eyes, was of greater stature. You cannot conceive what relief this admission was to me. My father not only gave me his permission, but his blessing. Oh, I shall weep again."

"And you shall live at Manydown, after all?" asked Cassandra.

"Yes. What could be more fortunate? My father has provided us with a large section of Manydown Park, and Heathcote and he have arranged for a London architect to build a manor house for us. We mean to marry next month, so we shall live elsewhere until it is completed. But that does not signify. The important thing is that I shall always be at Manydown, and that Heathcote shall always be with me."

This brought her nearly to tears once more, but she recovered as they approached Manydown House.

"Ah, my dears, how good it is to see you again," said Mr. Bigg-Wither. "I trust you have had your share of diversions in Bath. Shall you be content now in dreary old Steventon, or have you been spoilt forever?"

"Quite the contrary, sir," said Jane. "Bath

could not possibly be more dreary for me than it was. How I longed for my home and friends. I could never be induced to go there again, if I could help it."

"I hope you were not ill, Jane. Or Cassandra. What could be the matter?"

"In short, I was sick of everything. Elegant gentlemen, women of fashion and condescension, insipid assemblies, shops no one could afford, theater performances whose sense could not be made out because of the noisy gossips. All of it infuriating," said Jane.

This effusion came with more vehemence than anyone, including Jane, could have predicted. Jane had known that the reason her mother and Aunt Leigh-Perrot conspired to take her to Bath was to find her a husband. That resentment had not diminished. Nor had the humiliation of Mr. Thackney having been paid to dance with her diminished. Jane strongly resented being patronized, especially by her aunt, who enjoyed feeling superior to her poor relations.

It was now Cassandra's turn to come to Jane's aid.

"As for me, Bath is no place for one in mourning. I was bored without my own home comforts. But, what a wonderful scene to return to here. We congratulate you heartily on the engagement of Lizzy and Heathcote."

"Oh, you cannot conceive how gratified I am," said Mr. Bigg-Wither. "My own dear Lizzy and Heathcote. And they shall be here at Manydown. I am more happy than I ever hoped to be, as I even deserve to be after my own catastrophic romantic excursion. Never again. Never again, I say. Marriage is for the young."

This lament struck new pangs in the hearts of both Jane and Cassandra, from which neither could rescue the other. Catherine was left to pick up the remains.

"Surely you speak only for yourself, Papa. Many second, and even third, marriages, when well considered, at any age, can be happy. The real problem is what women are to do who do not wish to marry at all."

"And why would they not, my dear? The advantage is all on their side," said Mr. Bigg-Wither.

"Dear Papa, you do not consider what it means to be a wife," said Catherine. "Only think. She gives her entire fortune to her husband, and is then forced into childbearing. Some women may not consider these to be advantages."

"Well, of course, these are valid considerations. But on the balance, taken on the whole, to be protected for life, to raise children, to be mistress of a comfortable home, to be loved, to be admired in society, is this not of more advantage?" asked Mr. Bigg-Wither.

"Only if she wishes it. If she does not, it is a punishment," said Catherine.

No one was certain where to direct the

conversation next. One could say that if a woman *does* wish it, then being deprived of it is a punishment, too, but no one would say it.

"That leaves adoption, does it not, Papa?" said Catherine, smiling at him in jest. "I have long thought we should adopt both Jane and Cassandra into the family."

"You are, indeed, like family. But consider, what an odd circumstance that would be. It is done frequently, to be sure, like your brother Edward. But do you not lose him? Does he not lose you? What value can be placed on such circumstances? Here is a moral question for Heathcote. He will know how to answer it."

Chapter 25

In early November of that year, Mr. and Mrs. Lefroy were discussing an upcoming visit of Tom Lefroy to Ashe Rectory after a two-and-one-half-year absence.

"Only think, Mr. Lefroy, how he will marvel over how our children are grown."

"And, perhaps, at how we, ourselves, have grown old," said Mr. Lefroy.

"Oh, I think not. Two years is nothing at our age. But *he* will have matured, undoubtedly, after two years of reading law, and his engagement to Miss Paul. He is a proper man now, where he was still a young man before."

"What say you on the subject of Jane Austen, madam? Has she made mention of Tom? Would she be grieved or happy to see him?"

"She has said nothing about him. After two years' time, she will have forgotten him. But, I would not like to give her pain, if it can be avoided. Surely, there can be no occasion for Tom to see her now," said Madam Lefroy. "He may not like to, either."

"Agreed. We shall celebrate his marriage only among ourselves. But what if the Austens learn of his visit by chance? I would not like it thought that we concealed the event. No, we had better mention it to some of our neighbors as a brief family visit."

"Jane would then surely become aware of it," said Madam Lefroy. "And then when Tom does not pay her a visit, she will know that nothing further is to be expected, if she ever had expectations. Do not mention that Tom is engaged, however. That would cause pain whether or not any attachment remains."

A few days later, while Mr. Austen was sitting alone with Jane in the parlor, he mentioned that Tom Lefroy was arriving at Ashe Rectory the following week for a visit. He was careful not to put too fine a point on it, since he remembered Jane's attention to Tom several years ago, and how altered Jane had been at his departure.

"Oh, Papa! Are you quite certain? Do you plan to visit them?"

"I think not, my dear. I comprehend that it is to be a visit of short duration. Private, I believe."

"Oh. And what do you suppose is the occasion? What could he mean by it? He has not visited for several years, you know."

"No doubt he wishes to renew the acquaintance of his uncle and aunt and nieces, especially now that his legal studies in London have concluded. He may not have had sufficient time before."

"Yes, I am certain you are right. Well. And you believe you would impose if you were to visit?"

"Quite certain. I should not think of it."

"Of course. I wonder whether mother will think of it."

"I shall advise her against it, my dear. It is to

be a quiet family time."

"Yes, I see. Of course."

What could this mean? Now that Tom's studies were over, and he was ready to begin a new life, had he finally come back for her? Could all the waiting have finally come to a happy end? Could she dare to hope for it? What other reason could there be for his visit now? And it was to be private. Perhaps that meant that were she to refuse him, he could retreat quickly without losing face, with a minimum of awkwardness.

Cassandra was at this time in Godmersham, staying with Edward and managing the household while his wife recuperated from childbirth. She was not expected to return for several months.

Oh, how I wish Cassandra were not forever being farmed out whenever some unfortunate relation is brought to bed of a child, thought Jane. How can she tolerate such abuse? Cassandra is too compliant, but she does seem to like caring for children. Still, it is an inconvenience to our own home. I am sick of the domestic duties when she is away. The kitchen help is surly, and my mother seems never to be well. Quite provoking.

But what if he does not give me an offer? Well, my disappointment will be no worse than it has been these last two years. It has been my constant companion. And resentment, along with it. But, if Tom's intention *is* to come to me, oh, I believe any amount of misery might be overlooked. Perhaps I *have* despised his behavior at times. I shall tell him so. In good time.

The following week came and went without a visitor of any sort except Catherine Bigg, who took pity on Jane while Cassandra was away. Catherine did not know the full extent of Jane's misery, or the reason for it. She only knew that Jane seemed particularly in need of friendship, but did not care to leave Steventon Rectory because of her mother's health. Jane and Catherine spent pleasant afternoons in the garden, and talked a great deal about Lizzy and Heathcote, and Harris and Mr. Bigg-Wither.

By the second week, Jane was in a state of anxiety as she had never been in before. She could not seem to sit still to read, and writing was out of the question. And, she had seen enough of the garden to last her a lifetime. At last, she encouraged her mother to invite Madam Lefroy for an afternoon visit, which she soon did.

"Oh, Jane, I am glad you are at home. I have here a letter from Mr. Samuel Blackall," said Madam Lefroy. "You will remember him from last winter. He was particularly attentive to you, I believe. It seems he will be unable, after all, to visit us this winter. But, it does not signify. We shall amuse ourselves just as well."

There were interruptions of one sort or another all afternoon, making further discussion with Madam Lefroy impracticable. By the time Madam Lefroy took her leave, Jane's heart was as heavy as an iron ball. The tears welling in Jane's eyes forced her to turn away briefly as she said goodbye, but she did not think Madam Lefroy had noticed.

Now it was Jane who walked slowly up the stairs to her bed chamber and closed the door behind her. She gave in quietly to tears for the rest of the afternoon, and for more reasons than she could name. Everything was in a muddle, and every new thought provoked more tears. Here was another death in the family. Tom would never come for her. How could she have been so foolish as to think he would? She would never see him again. How could she bear the humiliation? She would never love again. She would be a spinster, to be pitied by all her friends and family forever. What would she live on? What was she to do?

She did not come down stairs all the rest of the next day, saying she had a headache, which she did. Everything ached, and nothing seemed worthwhile enough to rise for. Her father came to see her in the afternoon to read a little to her.

"I shall be better tomorrow, Papa. I promise you. I am not unwell. I am only very tired. I wish I had been able to speak more to Madam Lefroy when she was here. But I was tired."

"Ah, yes, Madam Lefroy is always good to talk to. I did inquire as to Tom Lefroy's visit, by the way. He only stayed a few days, and was off again to London on his way back to Ireland to practice the law. His family is prodigiously proud of him."

"Of course, and so they should be. His Uncle

Benjamin, too, I daresay."

"My dear, you are overwrought. A drop of your mother's laudanum would benefit you tonight. And you shall be quite a new woman in the morning."

"Yes, Papa. You are all goodness. You are the very soul of us all. I do not doubt it. I shall always remember your kindness to me."

"There, there, my dear. There is no occasion for all this sentimentality. You are my own dear child.",

But you, too, will die, and leave me, Papa, thought Jane. Oh, Cassandra. At least I will always have you.

Chapter 26

Seldom were both Cassandra and Jane from home at the same time, but such were the circumstances in early December of 1800. Conversation was thereby made unavoidable between Mr. and Mrs. Austen for several weeks together.

"What say you, Mrs. Austen, to the idea of retiring?" asked Mr. Austen one evening. "I am now almost seventy, and beginning to feel it. The fields and gardens and the dairy give satisfaction enough for a young man, but they grow increasingly dispiriting for an older one."

"Mr. Austen, you forget that your spirit is not the only consideration in the matter. There is mine, as well, to be sure."

"And that is the reason I put the question to you, in particular."

"Well, then, who would do the work, if not you? You are not suggesting that my work increase, surely."

"No, no, my dear. I have James in mind. He is ordained and ready to take on a parish living. He must be longing for a more permanent situation for his family. This home would naturally be passed to him, within the family."

"What? Do you mean we would be turned out of our home altogether? You can not be in earnest, sir. Why, where would we go? What will become of us? What would we live on?"

"The living does not provide for remuneration upon retirement. But if we live simply, which is all we require, after all, we may spend our time with family and friends for part of the year, and then rent a modest place for the other part. We could sell much of our furniture, which would provide a handsome sum."

"You mean we would be vagabonds! Poor relations no one wants to see coming down the lane. I would be mortified, Mr. Austen, and I fail to see how this idea could be satisfactory to you."

"Only consider, my dear, what must be your situation upon my demise, which cannot be many years hence. Nay, nay, hear my words, madam. You will have two grown daughters to provide for, in addition to yourself. Cassandra and Jane are not likely to marry from the neighboring villages. Their circle is not sufficiently varied. Removing to Bath more permanently must be to their advantage in life, and better sooner than later, to become acquainted with a greater number of families. We must do what we can to assist them.

"As for yourself, your health is indifferent enough that the prospect of managing this home, with all it entails, may become greater than you are equal to. And, consider, your own health may well improve by taking the waters more often. And then, would you not prefer to be nearer to your brother and Mrs. Leigh-Perrot? That could not be amiss if you require assistance, you know. There is much to be said for Bath, my dear, when all considerations are brought to bear."

"Ah, well. Had you mentioned Bath at the outset, I might not have brought protest. There is so much in the way of diversion, to be sure. And the families are, indeed, of a finer sort. For our girls. And, surely, our sons will do what they can to make matters easy. But, I should dearly miss what we have here, Mr. Austen. My gardens! I cannot bear it!"

"Perhaps a few days thought on the matter will help us both consider the best course," said Mr. Austen. "I comprehend how discomposing the suddenness of this subject may be. Shall we put it aside for the present?"

No, Mrs. Austen saw no occasion to put it aside so quickly now that the matter *had* been presented, for she had many questions to put to Mr. Austen. What of the servants? What of the animals? What of the carriage? She would not be easy until she could imagine the entire scene. And, would they absolutely be required to live simply? Would that even be possible in Bath? How much lower in society would they necessarily fall, especially as compared to her brother? These were matters of consequence.

By the time Cassandra and Jane were to return, the Austens had not only decided absolutely to retire and quit the rectory, but that Bath was by many degrees the best city in the world. Everyone would benefit. James and his family would have a stable living, Mr. Austen would be able to rest and read, Mrs. Austen would meet fine families and attend plays, and Cassandra and Jane would find husbands with fortunes. There were almost no reasons not to remove to Bath, except for the gardens, but they were quickly forgot.

So pleased were the Austens with the decision that they discussed it with James and his wife Mary, who were no less pleased. Indeed, James was heartily grateful, and shook his father's hand with both of his again and again, almost in disbelief at his benevolence. And Mary, who had a keen eye, looked around the rectory with a new perspective, considering which of the furniture she might like to keep. With an organizing mind, as well, Mary comprehended immediately which tasks and decisions must be undertaken, and which were dependent on other decisions. She would devise a written plan, which would make everything go smoothly.

Jane and Cassandra returned from their travels a few days later. The coach arrived earlier than expected in the afternoon, resulting in Mrs. Austen being their only welcoming party.

"Girls, girls, you are very welcome home. Let us have your bags brought inside, my dears, and then I must tell you a surprise. No, no, you can not guess it. It is quite unexpected and new."

Once in the parlor, with barely time to catch her breath, Mrs. Austen proceeded.

"My dears, what do you think? Our good Mr.

Austen is to retire at last. He shall be seventy soon, you know, and may not live for many more years. Therefore, we shall all remove to Bath! James and Mary shall have the rectory, and we shall have the time of our lives in a new and much better society. My health will surely improve. Is it not wonderful news? What say you?"

"Oh, Mamma!" cried Cassandra. "What can you mean by this? Are you ill, Mamma? Has anything happened? Do you know of what you speak? Surely, you are mistaken. Father would never give up our life here. He loves it as much as we do, I am certain."

Jane could not speak, but stared disbelievingly at her mother. The more Cassandra asked questions and was given answers, the more it did seem that her mother was in earnest. Jane slumped back on the sofa, completely helpless. Her eyes were closed as Cassandra noticed her suffering, and came to her aid.

"Jane, Jane, pray, do not be distressed. We shall speak to father when he returns straight away. He is a man of sense and compassion, is he not? He has never failed us, and never will. This cannot be true."

As she spoke and gently held Jane's hand, Jane at last opened her eyes and wept.

"Oh, Cassandra, what are we to do? Our life is being taken away. Do you not feel it?"

"Nonsense, Jane," said Mrs. Austen "Quite the contrary. You will at last be in superior company. Your lives will be much improved. That was a major consideration on our part in making this decision, I assure you. Only think of the fine assemblies and new friends and plays to attend. Do you want to waste away here all your lives? I should think you would show a little gratitude for what your father and I have done on your account.

"I was a little shocked, myself, when Mr. Austen presented the idea to me, I do admit. But, you shall soon come to see what a brilliant plan it is, as I did. And Mary is so very organized. You shall barely need to exert yourselves. She has been here nearly every day with her plans and papers, and has everything under control."

"Mary? What has she to do with it?" cried Jane. "Has she already made plans to replace you, Mamma? Do you not see what she does? Her grasping manner? Oh, for shame. It is insufferable. All of it. And, Bath! No, never. Anywhere except Bath!"

Mr. Austen, alas, came home to a house turned nearly upside down with recriminations, red faces, refusals, tears, pleadings, pacing of floorboards, and finally, running up the stairs and slamming the door. His heart was heavy, indeed. But his mind had not been altered. For this was the best chance he could give his girls to secure their future, even if they could not now see it.

Chapter 27

In early January, as many of the plans for removing and selling possessions were being made, Cassandra traveled to Godmersham again to Edward and his family, whom Cassandra considered her second family. Edward's wife Elizabeth had become Cassandra's particular friend, and all the children delighted her.

Cassandra did not seem to have the same deep sense of loss of Steventon Rectory as did Jane, who was now left not only with all of Cassandra's household duties, which she detested, but had to contend with the near constant presence of Mary in the home, as well, and the seizing of the family's possessions by her. Items that were not seized were sold. Furniture and paintings and manuscripts and music and books and animals and farm equipment were disposed of without Cassandra's or Jane's opinions being sought. However, Jane did finally resist when her mother and Cassandra suggested that her own cabinet should be given to her niece. She begged to be the one to decide when to be generous with her own things.

The whole world is in a conspiracy to enrich one part of our family at the expense of another, she wrote to Cassandra.

Jane spent as much time out of the house as she could, even in the snow, in order to avoid the continual interchange between her mother and

Mary. She had given strict instructions that no one was to so much as touch her writing box. She even put a sign on it to that effect in large letters. Every day when she returned from her wandering, something had been altered. A picture had been removed, leaving a brown square on the wall where a beautiful green landscape had lived since before she was born, now uprooted in the storm, as she was.

Her life was falling apart, and she had no control over it. Every day there was less and less of it. Had she ever had any control over it? She wondered. She had always been at others' mercy. When her father died, she would be dependent upon her brothers; unless she married, in which case, she would be dependent upon her husband. What was her destiny, after all?

She was to lose the only home she had known, lose most of her possessions, and be forced to remove to a place she could not love, a busy city rather than the peaceful country she needed in order to write, to a home that had not yet been found. All this, and Cassandra had distanced herself from her to a less disruptive home. Jane resented it all.

She had few comforting thoughts during this time, but one of them was that the seaside would be more convenient from Bath for holidays. Mr. Austen did agree that the family should travel to Devonshire immediately upon settling in Bath. For this, Jane was grateful, for she longed for the romance of the seaside, imagining the stories of sailors' wives waiting stoically amid the crashing waves on overcast days, their skirts flapping around their legs, and their hair blowing wildly around their faces.

In Bath, the Leigh-Perrots had agreed to house the Austens in May until a suitable home could be found for them. However, Mrs. Leigh-Perrot found difficulty being able to afford room and board for the four of them, despite being rich. To her mind, housing two Austens was sufficiently generous. Or at the most, three. But not four. For once, there existed a plausible reason for such parsimony: Mrs. Leigh-Perrot was in jail. She had been accused in August of the previous year of stealing lace from a millinery shop. The trial was scheduled for March, and the total cost of the arduous ordeal could not be calculated. That she was willing to house anyone under these circumstances was more remarkable than her limiting them to only two or three.

Given these circumstances, then, there were communications between the Austens that perhaps another place could be found for Jane since she was the least fond of Bath. To this, Jane replied that she did not want to be left behind, and that perhaps she could make herself ill by eating Bath buns, so that no further food would be required for her. Amused as she was to suggest this in a letter to Cassandra, her resentments grew daily. Her opinions about the removal had been inconsequential, she was left to contend with her mother and Mary without Cassandra's support, and now she seemed to be, in fact, entirely dispensable.

She attempted to soothe her growing indignation by writing, imagining new characters and scenes and plots in Bath for her new novel, called *Susan*, while her family made their plans.

At last, it was determined that Mr. Austen would travel to Thorpe alone to visit relatives for several weeks in May, and then would meet in Bath with the Leigh-Perrots, Mrs. Austen, and Jane. Cassandra was to visit the Fowles in Kintbury before coming at last to Bath. The Austens were then to travel together to Sidmouth in Devon at the seashore.

There were still four months to be endured while the rectory was being taken over, however. There were so many visitors and activities in January that Jane was relieved in February to visit Manydown, *her* second home. The distractions had been so continual that she had not been able to write very much in January, after all.

"I fear I am losing myself, Catherine. I know not what will become of me. I have no means of living without obeying my father. And when he is no more, I will have no means of living without obeying my brothers. This is not the life I had hoped for, nor am I certain what I hope for any more."

"I see what you are feeling," commiserated Catherine. "Without a husband, we are at the mercy of others' wishes."

"So are we with a husband. Only then, we may hope that our opinions matter. But that is by no means a certainty, either, I suppose."

They were sitting in the library, being warmed by the fireplace while the snow fell steadily outside the wide windows. There was no color beyond the library windows, only a blank, deep world of nothing in particular as far as Jane could see. This library, this house, this family, she would be leaving them all behind, as well.

When she had been a girl, she had imagined that when she grew up, her own house would look exactly like this library. There would be dark mahogany bookshelves from floor to ceiling on three of the walls, and a great stone fireplace with large old family paintings above it and on both sides. And then there would be a sturdy mahogany ladder that could reach to the top shelves, if she dared to climb that high.

"What had you hoped for, then?" asked Catherine.

"Something more. A greater meaning, somehow — or deeper. Or at least the means to achieve something of my own, to see what I can be. That's it, really. I can achieve nothing of my own except to duplicate myself with children. And those daughters will, in turn, be able to achieve nothing of their own. It is a cycle that reproduces itself only for its own sake, not for the sake of achieving anything worthwhile. The cycle must stop at some point for something new to occur. Some tangent, if you follow my meaning. Do you not agree?"

"I am not as adverse to marriage as you are. If I am unable to achieve something of my own, I will be pleased to raise children who themselves may be able to achieve more than I can. I could be quite content if I have made my family and my friends happy. That is what I hope for."

"Yes. I should be proud to say the same. But I cannot. Those are all important, but I cannot be content without something more, something of my own."

Mr. Bigg-Wither had come into the library now, and had settled himself in his enormous reading chair.

"Pray, when do you leave for Bath, Jane?" he asked.

"In May, I believe, sir. Our plans have undergone some changes, but that much seems certain now."

"And Cassandra, is she still at home?"

"No, she is at Godmersham, and will likely remain there until she goes to Kintbury. We shall join again in Bath."

"Oh, my dear, you must be feeling the loss. I am sorry to hear it all, as much as I esteem your father. If you wish it, we have here a home for you until May. You may well determine to remain at home as long as it is still yours, of course. I quite comprehend. But if you find that it helps you to be away, please consider the offer. You have friends here who care for you. Indeed, we do, my dear."

All was shortly settled. Jane was to stay at Manydown until the end of April, leaving everyone else to retire and plan and sell and seize and look after other peoples' children as they wished. Jane would stay away.

Chapter 28

The removal to Manydown brought many days of the long quiet hours Jane required for peace of mind and for writing. Mornings were devoted to visiting and being visited, which brought activity and liveliness to each day. That was a sufficient amount of social life, aside from the occasional winter ball, which Jane only half-heartedly attended with Catherine, Alethea, and Harris.

Mealtimes were a time to discuss projects and land and gardens and livestock, all of which Jane found interesting. She went on excursions daily, and took note of all the changes the end of winter and beginning of spring brought. She found the first violet crocus and snowdrops, and eagerly showed them to Catherine. And Mr. Bigg-Wither consulted her as well as Catherine on any subjects on which he needed to make decisions. He consulted the two of them more often than he did Harris, whose temperament and reason he found variable.

During the latter part of February, Catherine traveled to Basingstoke for a fortnight to visit friends, leaving Jane as mistress of the manor for a time, a situation she rather enjoyed. No household duties were required, since there were many servants.

Mr. Bigg-Wither was a quiet and thoughtful gentleman, easy to converse with, and amiable in every regard. And, he clearly admired Jane's good sense and liveliness. Of wit, he could not be her equal. But, he was encouraging of her need for solitude and for writing, thinking that she kept a diary, as many women did. It was a harmless, wholesome activity.

"How do your mother and father progress in their preparations for removal, Jane?" asked Mr. Bigg-Wither one day.

"I received a letter yesterday from my mother, saying that I would barely recognize the rectory now. So much furniture has been removed that the rooms stand almost empty. And Mary and James have made themselves at home. It seems all goes well, according to their plans."

"Do you wish to return for a visit?"

"No. My memories are too fond to have them shaken just now. I wish to keep them intact as long as possible. I know not what lies ahead, and so I must fortify myself with my memories, at least. My stay here has helped to that end, sir, more than I can express. I am deeply grateful for your hospitality. Manydown is all steadiness and comfort for me."

"Oh, pray do not imagine that I was searching for gratitude by my inquiry. It is my particular pleasure to have you here, Jane. You have brought happiness and laughter to all of us at various times. Your removal to Bath will be an occasion of sorrow for us. Elizabeth and Heathcote inquire after you in their letters, and Catherine will lose her lifelong friend. Even Harris has mentioned that it will be a loss to him."

"You are all very good. I am comforted to know that Manydown will always be here. And, as for Bath, well, I may grow to like it, after all. It has its charms. Do you like Bath, particularly?" asked Jane.

"The occasional visit suits me. Going to a play and drinking the waters are all very well, but I am soon tired of it and longing for home. Indeed, I have been chided for not taking my girls and Harris there for every season in order to meet the right families. But I am of the opinion that meeting the right families is not as important as having the right friends, those we have known, families we have known, people we care about. Superior gentlemen like Heathcote are not likely to be found wandering about Bath for the season. Nor are superior gentlewomen, for that matter."

"I believe you are right, sir."

"You do not find me so very out-of-date in my thinking, then?"

"No, not at all. I agree with you," said Jane.

This was as far as Mr. Bigg-Wither dared to take this subject for one day. He had grown very fond of Jane over the years, and lately, had even wondered whether it would possible to secure her for his wife. He was much older, being now fifty-nine to Jane's twenty-five. But such an age difference was not unheard of, especially when the woman was beyond her initial bloom. It seemed to him that Jane could benefit from having an established home among people who loved her. And her lack of a fortune did not signify in the least, for his own was vast. Yes, the idea had a great deal of merit.

Chapter 29

Catherine returned to Manydown in March, refreshed from her travels, and eager to now spend time with Jane for the two remaining months until Jane was to remove to Bath. She found Jane very much more at ease than she had been a few weeks earlier.

"How I have missed you, Catherine. How was your journey?" asked Jane as Catherine came in the house from the cold and removed her heavy cloak.

"A bit chilly and bumpy, actually. But, I was gladdened by all the new wildflowers along the way. They were not blooming when I left. Spring is coming. Is it not remarkable that it occurs every year? Some years, like this one, when there have been deep frosts, I wonder whether it has not been too bad for anything to try to ever grow again. It is foolish, I know. But, really, is it not the most extraordinary thing?"

"It is," laughed Jane. "And not foolish at all. Last week when I was walking, I suddenly smelled spring, just for a moment. There seemed to be a waft of wind coming from somewhere that reminded me of new-mown hay, although, of course, that could not be. It was extraordinary. It altered my feelings. I had been thinking somewhat darkly, I will admit, of what I am to endure in Bath, and where I shall live. But then I began thinking beyond Bath, towards

Sidmouth on the coast. How fresh and welcome will be the beaches and waves. I would much prefer to live there than Bath. But I know it cannot be since it is meant for holidays. The costs cannot be thought of. Have you ever been to Sidmouth?" asked Jane.

"Not that I recall, but I understand it is beautiful in the summer. I would not care for it in winter, I am certain. The cold and damp must be frightful."

"Perhaps," said Jane. "But still I believe I would prefer it to Bath."

"I believe you would prefer any place to Bath. Pray, if you could live anywhere in England, excepting Steventon, where would you live?"

"That would depend entirely on my fortune. If I had one of my own, I would chose somewhere on the coast: Lyme Regis, Exeter, Sidmouth, or somewhere near there. But as it is, I am at the mercy of others. Therefore, the grander, the better," Jane laughed. "Godmersham is very grand, to be sure. I love Manydown, of course."

They came into the drawing room, where Harris was writing a letter. Here was the glory of Mrs. Croft's redecorating talents on full display. The soft green brocade sofas (Mr. Collier had chosen the fabric) were meant for conversations. It was a bright room with lit sconces on the wall and large house plants gracing the corners.

"W-W-Welcome home, Kitty. It is high time you returned and took your r-r-rightful place as mistress of our humble abode again. Poor Jane has had to make all manner of d-d-decisions in your absence," said Harris.

"Why could *you* not make decisions? Are you not qualified?" asked Catherine.

"Hardly. When it comes to the p-pantry, I am an expert only on what is to be taken out, not what is to be b-brought in. And when it comes to the chickens, I c-care not what happens to them at all. They are to be k-killed and eaten, after all, so their daily care cannot be of much c-consequence. I leave that to others," said Harris.

"Father may wish for you to share the responsibility of Manydown, since you are to inherit it. Do you not wish to…"

"Yes, I do wish to inherit Manydown, but I see no occasion to become m-mistress of the house when you are away. That is what I meant," said Harris.

"You see, Jane, he is a hopeless case, is he not?" asked Catherine.

"As it happens, Kitty," added Harris, "J-Jane has been an excellent mistress of the house."

Jane rolled her eyes to the ceiling.

"I have no doubt she has," said Catherine. "Let us leave this good-for-nothing alone to his letter-writing before he finds a way to have us do it for him," said Catherine, leading Jane upstairs so Catherine could put away her things. She had many more trunks for her fortnight away than Jane had for her four-month stay. Jane sat on her bed while Catherine refolded her gowns.

"My father writes wonderful letters to me when I am away," said Catherine when she and Jane were alone. "He is such a dear, you know. In his last letter, he mentioned his concern about your future, how he wishes he could do more for you. Do you remember a long time ago, we joked how amusing it would be if my father were to marry you?"

"Yes, and I remember you cried 'Never'," laughed Jane. "It would be absurd for me to be your step-mamma. We are almost sisters, after all."

"But if that awkwardness could somehow be sorted out, Jane..." said Catherine, more seriously now. "What I mean is, could you ever consider...you know, marrying my father? Is it completely out of the question?"

"Oh, Catherine. Has he asked you for my hand? How very odd is this conversation."

"No, no, of course not. How shocking that would be. La! What an idea."

"But what, then, can you mean by it? Are you suggesting that your father has an attachment to me?" asked Jane.

"Well, he likes you, certainly. He has not said so directly. But only think, Jane. You would be mistress of Manydown. You would never have to go to Bath if you do not like it. You would never want for anything again. We could still be sisters. Do you see? Could you care for him, Jane? That is the main thing. He is a goodhearted man, I promise you. He treated my mother like a queen. But could you be happy? Or not?"

"I have no idea. How can you talk so? Is this a prank that Harris has thought up, by chance? Ah, I see it. Most amusing. Really, Catherine."

"No, no. Jane, pray do not dismiss the idea just now. We shan't discuss it again, if you do not like it. But will you think about it to yourself? Only to yourself. Just say that you will, and only you shall choose to speak of it again. Will that do? Pray, say yes," said Catherine.

"I shall think about it to myself, yes. But is that what you would want? Truly? How have you come to change your opinion?" asked Jane.

"I do not know, exactly. I suppose it gradually occurred to me that the idea would make everybody happy. Even Harris."

"What? You do not mean to say that you have discussed this with Harris," said Jane.

"Oh, no. Of course not. I only mean that he would likely give his approbation to such a match."

"How can you say so? Would it not delay his inheritance of Manydown?" asked Jane.

"Not at all. It is entailed through the male line, so the estate would be his regardless of whether father marries."

"What, then, would be my fate when your father is gone? I would be penniless and on the streets."

"No, no. Undoubtedly, my father would provide handsomely for you in his will at the time of your marriage."

"Catherine, I beg you will now stop this subject, for I know not what to say or what to think about it. I am much indebted to you for all your hospitality towards me. Indeed, I am. But I am to remain here another two months, and I would not wish for you to look upon me daily in anticipation of a decision on my part. The only decision I can make is to remove to Bath with my family. I may amaze everyone and become enamored with it. At the least, I will have the benefit of some distance in order to consider it carefully without influence."

"I comprehend you, Jane. I would not wish to distress you. You already have much to consider."

"And, of course, I should not like to delay my holiday in Sidmouth," said Jane, smiling.

She did think of the idea to herself. This could be her home. These many comfortable bed chambers, the warm library with its tall windows, the elegant parlor, all the staircases and tapestries, the stables, lawns, gardens, and woods. Here would be peace and stability in the country she loved, among people she cared for and who cared for her. Cassandra could perhaps make this her home, too. And Jane could most likely continue to write.

Considering all this, was it too fine a point that she did not love Mr. Bigg-Wither? She would not be the first woman nor the last to marry for convenience. Could she come to love him? She would never be in love again as she had been with Tom. That much was certain.

Chapter 30

In the first week of May, 1801, Mrs. Austen and Jane arrived together at The Paragon in Bath, where the Leigh-Perrots were both residing, Mrs. Leigh-Perrot having been acquitted of the charge of theft in March. Neither Cassandra nor Mr. Austen were to present themselves before June, leaving Jane in more sour company than she could wish for. Both Mrs. Austen and her aunt had colds, and kept each other entertained comparing their symptoms every day.

Jane's days were spent in visiting houses to let with her mother, aunt, and uncle, which Jane rather enjoyed. Seldom had she seen how strangers lived in a city. There was no end of cramped quarters, hideous wallpaper, rising damp, and ill-favored views.

As for the social life, it had mercifully diminished with the end of the season, providing Jane deliverance from meeting important families and elegant gentlemen. She soon tired of the few she could not avoid.

There was one last ball at the assembly rooms, however, which Jane attended with some amusement, spotting a known adulteress with a little too much rouge, and watching the spectacle of an inebriated woman chasing her equally inebriated husband around the assembly rooms.

But, Jane's mind was almost invariably

distracted at Bath. All her belongings in Steventon were being sold by Mary and James, for how much she did not know. If she had been asked why the value mattered, she would, perhaps, have said that it was because her family were in want of ready cash. But, she also wondered at her own value, having now been separated from her possessions. All she had left of value, really, was herself and her manuscripts.

Her value to Cassandra had certainly diminished. Cassandra had abandoned her for five months when Jane needed her most. And, Cassandra must have known that Jane would perceive this as abandonment, since they had often talked about such feelings. But in her letters, Jane was careful not to allow her pain to surface for fear of driving Cassandra farther away. Jane was still at everyone's mercy, physically and emotionally, and getting smaller and smaller, and angrier and more resentful.

Her relationship with her father had also diminished since his decision to remove from the rectory. He could not sympathize with her need for the peacefulness of Steventon, for he was convinced she was wasting her life and would never find a husband. As for her mother…there was no real diminishment there, for Jane could never depend on her for emotional support.

She missed her home, but she did not actually wish to return there any more, knowing that the rooms had been turned upside-down, someone else had taken residency in her bed chamber, and every dear image and remaining object was now altered forever. The last five months at Manydown had taught her to accept the finality of the rectory.

But she did feel the pull of Manydown every day. It was the one place in which she now felt wanted and supported and at peace. Had she not longed for the seaside so fervently, she could have insisted on returning, and taken on a new life there by agreeing to marry Mr. Bigg-Wither. But she decided to go forward — at least for this one next trip. Then she would consider again what to do.

At last, Mr. Austen and Cassandra arrived together on June 1st, with all the celebration attendant on the occasion. The two of them had visited the home of the Fowles in Kintbury, and Cassandra had received the one thousand pounds bequeathed to her from the will Tom Fowle had made before going to the West Indies.

Jane had become used to having her own bed chamber all during May in Bath, and since January before that in Manydown. She now found that she preferred her privacy, and bade her aunt to make other bed chamber arrangements for Cassandra, which could easily be accommodated.

"Oh, dear Jane, it is wonderful to see you, at last," said Cassandra. "We have both experienced much in these last few months, and I have missed talking with you every day. How shall we ever make up the time?"

"Ah, Cassandra. Do you not know that time is the one thing we can never recover?"

"Of course, you are right, and we have lost a good deal of it. I am sorry for it, indeed."

Jane now turned and found that she had other questions for her father about his trip. In truth, she was only partially engaged in his conversation, for her sensibilities were much agitated by her words with Cassandra. She was aware of having given her sister pain deliberately, and alternated between feeling quite justified and feeling sorry. But, no, she was very angry, and Cassandra must feel it. She would not allow such misuse to be passed over lightly, to be forgotten with a trivial apology. This was no trivial matter, and Cassandra would be made to comprehend its significance.

Later in the evening, Cassandra asked Jane to accompany her on a short walk for some exercise.

"I fear you are cross with me, Jane, for having stayed away too long. I would not have it so," began Cassandra.

"But you *would* have it so," said Jane, deliberately misconstruing Cassandra's meaning. "It was your doing, and your decision. No one forced you to stay while I was asking you to return. How could you do it, Cassandra? How could you leave me in that chaos, with mother and James and Mary? I know not how I shall ever forgive you. I know not that you shall ever deserve to be forgiven, either. Such a sister, indeed!"

"This is more than I can bear, Jane," said Cassandra, starting now to cry.

"And did you know what I was able to bear? Did you give it thought?"

"Yes, yes, of course, I did. Truly, Jane, I cannot entirely account for my behavior. It was selfish of me, I own."

"It was more than selfish of you, it was hurtful to *me*. That is what you have not owned," said Jane. "What could you mean by it? What have I done to deserve such abuse from you?"

"Nothing, nothing, dear Jane. You have been ever faithful to me. I am much aware that you have always looked upon me as almost a mother. I feel it deeply, pray believe me. But you are now five and twenty. You are no longer a child in constant need of protection by an older sister."

"Ah, I see," said Jane, stopping now to face Cassandra. "I had not considered it to be protection. I had considered it to be kindliness and sisterly friendship. There is where we differ, I believe."

"Where we differ, Jane, is in our ages. You would feel this if you were the elder. Only consider. Would you not feel always responsible for your younger sister, with no possibility of an independent life, unless you or your sister could marry?"

"Oh, oh! For shame, Cassandra! Have I, then, prevented your happiness by not marrying? Pray, say no more. You know better than anyone how I have suffered. Every word from you is a fresh dagger."

"I only hope, Jane, that you will reconsider and forgive me. I did not wish to hurt you, but I own that I did. I am very sorry, indeed."

Whether she was or not did not concern Jane at the moment, for she was too distraught. Yes, there was much now to reconsider, but Jane was more hurt and angry than she had ever been.

Jane turned to go back, walking quickly, several steps ahead of Cassandra.

Chapter 31

The weeks in May spent searching for living quarters in Bath were not entirely misspent. By June, when Mr. Austen and Cassandra joined the party, much had been learned in the way of suitable locations, building construction, and prospects. One other benefit now presented itself: with the arrival of Mr. Austen, the Leigh-Perrots were not absolutely required to accompany them on their searches.

"What luck that my cold has let up a little," said Mrs. Austen. "For I would not have been equal to this manner of driving around before you arrived, Mr. Austen. I was quite poorly. Was I not, Jane?"

"To be sure, Mamma. We are fortunate to have you back among the able-bodied. Now we may at last look in earnest and decide. We did not want to choose anything you did not like, Papa. For my part, it can all not come quickly enough. I am already sick of Bath, and long to be at the seashore."

The week ended in success, for very suitable apartments were at last discovered at No.4 Sydney Place. Within a few days, the removal carriages had brought the beds Mrs. Austen had not been able to part with, along with the few other belongings no one else had seized or sold. The family was snug and in one place, at last.

"How gratified I am, Mr. Austen, that we are

settled," said Mrs. Austen, "and that our new home is not terribly shabby. I did have some concerns on that score when you first mentioned Bath, for I was advised by Madam Lefroy that we should find lodgings very dear. Even my sister does not think Sydney Place very far down in society.'

"And that is all I live for, Mamma," said Jane.

"I am pleased to hear you say so, my dear, for you have been somewhat indifferent to the matter," replied Mrs. Austen.

"Now, let us come to agreement on our holiday," said Mr. Austen. "I have drawn here a map for our travels. Sidmouth is to be our destination. But, we may take the most southerly route from here, and then travel further south along the coast towards Sidmouth. What say you to that, girls?"

"Oh, yes, Papa," said Cassandra. "By all means. Lyme Regis could be our first stop. How I long to see it."

"Oh, but Mr. Austen, that will not do. We must go to Totnes first, to be sure. Do you not recall my letter on the matter?"

Alas, Mr. Austen did not.

"How can you be so forgetful, sir? I wrote to you that Dr. John Blackall at Totnes is exceptionally fine at diagnosis and the dropsy, which, you know, I suffer from exceedingly. Madam Lefroy made special mention of that to me before we were to leave. She said, 'Do not fail to consult Dr. Blackall in Totnes, Mrs. Austen, upon any account. He shall cure you of all your complaints.'"

"Could we but hope for such a miracle?" asked Jane.

"My dear," said Mr. Austen, "I beg you would allow me to converse with your mother on this matter."

"I beg pardon, Papa. However, it is very hard upon us who do not suffer exceedingly from dropsy to delay a much wished-for holiday, when my mother has complained of dropsy for these ten years together."

Cassandra drew Jane away a little as this discussion was gaining heat.

"Consider, Jane," she whispered, "that we shall never have quiet until she has consulted the doctor. We may delay a few days, but that is not long when considering the entire summer. And if the doctor can bring her relief, I believe that will bring us all a measure of peace."

There was some truth to this.

"I am shocked at you, Jane!" cried Mrs. Austen. "You would deny your own mother treatment for her condition in favor of a summer holiday? What sort of creature have we raised up, Mr. Austen? That is what I wish to know."

"I beg you would excuse me, Mamma," said Jane. "Certainly you must have whatever treatments Dr. Blackall finds necessary for your present relief. Let us, then, proceed to Totnes directly. You are quite right. I regret my impatience, Mamma."

A few days later, Mr. Austen had reorganized his map while the women had packed and repacked their trunks for their summer holiday, fretting over the state and color of every bonnet.

The Leigh-Perrots kindly invited the Austens for dinner on their last evening in Bath, with a view towards advising them on the most scenic routes, and on whomever the Leigh-Perrots were acquainted with in every town.

"Certainly you shall travel through Taunton," said Aunt Leigh-Perrot. "We are much acquainted with the Claridges there, who are quite prominent in the city. They will provide whatever hospitality you require if you but mention our names."

The Austens were grateful for all these recommendations, and Mr. Austen duly wrote all the names and cities in his notebook. On this subject, however, all four of the Austens had similar unspoken thoughts. They would need to be in dire straits, indeed, to look up any of them, for who would wish to be connected with the name of Leigh-Perrot? The disgraceful incident and trial of the alleged theft of the lace by Mrs. Leigh-Perrot only a few months prior must surely be discomfiting. Only Mrs. Leigh-Perrot was unaware of this probability.

In the morning, the Austen's first coach was boarded, heading south toward Totnes, with much relief to all. They had undergone enormous changes in the first half of the year. That was all now behind them, and a bold new adventure was to begin.

Chapter 32

The trip to Totnes was to take four days. Mrs. Austen was reminded often of her dropsy symptoms since she was shortly to consult with an expert doctor. She did not want to forget any of them for fear of neglecting to list them all to him. The other three Austens were much less talkative, each entertaining thoughts of their own.

They were very fortunate in the weather. After a somewhat rainy month of May, what a pleasure it was to now see the masses of wildflowers and blooming trees in the fresh sunshine along the sides of the roads.

This was the country, after all, with green rolling hills in the distance, ancient stone bridges over quiet streams, and stately groves of trees. Through one hamlet after another, they could see dairymaids carrying their buckets along the lanes, schoolboys playing among the hedges, men driving their cows and carts, and groups of women talking and waving as the coach rattled past on the uneven gravel. Jane thought she could happily live among them forever.

"Dr. Blackall is the brother of an admirer of yours, Jane," said Mrs. Austen, just on the outskirts of Totnes.

"Oh? How came you not to tell me of this before?"

"Madam Lefroy was uncertain whether this

would be of consequence to you since you showed so very little interest in him in the past. But, I thought now I might as well tell you as not, since we are almost in Totnes. Do you recall Reverend Samuel Blackall from four years ago? Madam Lefroy was hoping for a match, you know. She has such a knack for those sorts of things."

"I remember him well, Mamma. Excessively talkative, but very agreeable, I thought. And very entertaining. I liked him well enough, but, at last, he did not show promise. I know not why."

"Madam Lefroy led me to believe that he has never forgotten you, and wishes he could have made a closer connection to the family. There! Did you know of this?"

"I knew a little of it, but I failed to understand why, if there was an attraction, he did not visit. I doubted his sincerity if he could not exert himself to make the slightest attempt."

Mrs. Austen was not known for her ability to manage secrets well. She therefore struggled mightily within the closed area of the coach to change the subject of discussion, for she had wandered very close.

"Ah, well. I know not whether you shall see him in Totnes. I rather think not."

Their coach entered Totnes late in the afternoon, allowing the Austens to put up at the Waterman's Inn to refresh themselves before visiting Dr. Blackall the next day.

Chapter 33

All four Austens visited Dr. Blackall's consulting office in Totnes the next day, for Mrs. Austen would not be left behind if there was to be sightseeing or shopping. However, as the rooms were not large, the Misses Austens waited outside on one of the wooden benches along the lane. The breeze brought familiar scents of flowers and grasses, with a little of horses and newly chopped wood, reminding them of the country and farms of Steventon. The citizens there were equally as welcome, looking not the least as if they had any of the pretensions of Bath, thought Jane.

People made entrances to Dr. Blackall's office all the morning, and came out again to wait on the benches next to Jane and Cassandra. One such person was a remarkably handsome man of about their age. He sat on a bench to the side of them, an angle making it awkward for them to see him properly. But there was something about him that Jane recognized: something in the manner of walking, and in his features. This could not be Samuel Blackall, certainly, for four years could not be sufficient to transform him all the way to handsome.

"He looks a little like Samuel Blackall, I daresay," whispered Jane. "Much more handsome, however, and much more quiet!"

"Say no more, Jane. Let us have no spectacles

here."

Jane held her tongue, but her curiosity was much aroused. And so it remained until Mr. and Mrs. Austen emerged at last from the office, accompanied by Dr. Blackall, himself."

"Dr. Blackall, allow me to introduce to you my daughters," began Mr. Austen. "Miss Austen, and Miss Jane Austen."

As Jane and Cassandra arose to be introduced to the doctor, the handsome man rose also.

"Welcome to Totnes," said Dr. Blackall. "It is quite a pleasure to meet you both. You have traveled a long distance, I believe. The hospitality at Waterman's Inn, I trust, has been satisfactory?"

"Oh, yes," answered Cassandra. "We are quite refreshed, I thank you. And we are all extremely grateful that you have been able to attend to our mother."

"The pleasure is mine, I assure you. And we have reason to be optimistic, as well, for I believe the few treatments I have given shall give her much relief. She is now to have a very pleasant holiday."

"Oh, allow me to introduce to you my brother, Thomas Blackall. He visits me this week, and then has holiday plans at the seashore."

"Good day, sir," said Mr. Austen. "We are most pleased to make your acquaintance. Are you a doctor, then, same as your brother?"

"No, sir," said Thomas. "One in the family is generally sufficient. I am a man of the cloth, myself.

A clergyman, from Exeter. And I am most pleased to make your acquaintance," he said, looking at all four of them.

"You are a fortunate man, Mr. Austen. What a fine portrait the four of you make standing just there. I should like to make a sketch to capture it, but my talent is woefully lacking. I hope to practice it at the shore in order to improve. Seascapes, I believe, are better suited to amateurs."

He was as affable and charming as every gentleman ought to be, thought Jane.

"Do you leave today, sir," asked Dr. Blackall, "or do you stay in Totnes?"

"We have no specific times appointed, since we did not know what Mrs. Austen's condition and treatment should require."

"In that case, I should be pleased to invite your family to my home for supper this evening, if that is convenient. Mrs. Blackall quite enjoys making a fuss for visitors."

"I can attest to that," said Thomas. "She treats me as a prince whenever I visit."

"But will Mrs. Blackall not be inconvenienced with so many visitors at short notice?" asked Mrs. Austen.

"Not at all, I assure you," said Dr. Blackall. "She has become accustomed to my wont of inviting people to our home. Our larder is kept quite full for all occasions. I hope you shall enjoy the evening."

"We can hardly refuse such a kind offer, doctor," said Mr. Austen, looking to Mrs. Austen and Jane and Cassandra for approbation, which they heartily gave. "Yes, we shall be very pleased to accept your offer."

After providing the necessary details for the evening, plus suggestions for spending the day in Totnes, the Blackall brothers bade them farewell.

"Oh!" cried Mrs. Austen, a safe distance away. "I am quite overtaken!"

"Are you unwell, my dear? Shall we return?" asked Mr. Austen.

"No, no, I am quite well. But, have you ever seen such a handsomer man in your life, girls? It is hard for a woman of modesty to have her legs examined quite so closely by such a man!"

"Do you mean besides Papa?" asked Jane. "Otherwise, I should not admit of it."

"Yes, yes, besides Mr. Austen, to be sure. But, what manners, and what a vast deal of knowledge upon all matters of physic. I feel quite well again."

"As do I, Mamma, and he did not once looked at my legs, that I am aware of," said Jane.

"I should be shocked, Jane, if he had. How can you say so? But, what say you to Mr. Thomas Blackall? He did not mention a wife, you know."

"He is an angel, Mamma," said Cassandra. "Are you not thankful, now, that we have come to Totnes, Jane? Only think. We may have missed their acquaintance altogether."

"Yes, I am nearly speechless," said Jane. All her senses were in such a state that confusion was the result.

"Well, I hope you will all recover by this evening," said Mr. Austen, "for I am most interested in seeing more of them. There are two men worth knowing, I daresay."

It now occurred to Jane, through the tangle in her head, that it was possible that Samuel Blackall could also be of the party that evening. Could he also be on holiday? And was that the real reason Dr. Blackall had invited them to supper? Oh, and had Madam Lefroy been responsible for this scene of meeting Samuel again? Perhaps his situation had changed, and he now wished to become reacquainted with her. Within a few steps along the lane, Jane's elation had taken a turn towards dread. But there was no escaping it now.

Chapter 34

At seven that evening, Thomas Blackall pulled up to Waterman's Inn in Dr. Blackall's carriage to retrieve the Austens, all of whom were fatigued from sightseeing for the better part of the day.

Dr. and Mrs. Blackall met them at their door, along with three beaming young children, one of whom held a large pet rabbit. What a scene of a happy family, thought Jane. No sooner had the Austens crossed the threshold of the house than they felt enveloped in the family, welcomed into the unceremonious world of an active home, with even the cook welcoming them heartily.

What a change from Bath,thought Jane. Her dread was soon banished, not least by the absence of Samuel. Everything was made easy. The children were well-mannered, but by no means dull as were so many over-disciplined children of the day. They waited to be noticed, but were as sweet as imaginable. The rabbit had to be patted, of course, before receiving his own supper of lettuce, carrots, and a bit of bread in his cage outside the back of the house, which Jane and Cassandra were invited to inspect.

The Austens had brought with them some buns and cakes from a bakery in town. These little gifts were warmly received and placed at the center of the table for everyone.

"How lucky for us that you came to Totnes. We would have felt quite sad to have missed meeting you, had you not been prevailed upon to join us here," said Mrs. Blackall.

Normally, such an effusion from a hostess would have caused Jane to raise her eyebrows. But from so guileless and open a countenance, one could only wish to be more like her, an effect not often experienced by Jane.

"And do you travel further tomorrow, Miss Austen?" asked Thomas, who was seated next to Cassandra.

"We hope to reach Teignmouth. It has been so long since we have been to the sea, I will be quite content wherever we go, so long as it should be spent traveling in sight of it," said she.

"Ah, it is quite another world. One that must refresh all who have the luxury of time for a holiday. The sand, the waves, the vastness of the view, it brings one to thoughts of the eternal and to reflect upon our lives, does it not?" asked Thomas. He had slowly shifted this question from Cassandra to Jane, who sat across from him.

"I cannot say, sir. My last experience of it was so long ago that there could not have been much life upon which to reflect. But, that must now be something to experience. I have, however, determined not to be content until I have placed at least two toes in the water. My expectations are quite humble, you see," said Jane, at which everyone laughed.

"You and your family will also be traveling, sir?" asked Mr. Austen. This was as sly a question as he was capable of. By the end of the evening, all the Austens had imagined Thomas to be a likely suitor to either Jane or Cassandra, but whether he had a family had not yet been determined.

"My brother's family is my family, as you see. But I shall be traveling to Sidmouth in a few weeks to visit an old friend whose health has become uncertain."

"Why, that is our destination, as well. Perhaps we shall see you there," said Mrs. Austen, now quite perked up by this development. "We plan to be there until the end of August. What a happy coincidence."

"I should be delighted, truly. Sidmouth is, of all places, a perfect little fishing village. Whenever I am there, I feel that I have always been a part of it. That I share its history, somehow. Yes, I hope we shall meet there, on the Esplanade," said Thomas, being careful to encompass all the Austens. This was not easily done, since they were not all together, so the effort was noticeable to anyone who was looking carefully, as both Jane and Cassandra were.

In the parlor after dinner, the oldest child played a little folk tune on the pianoforte that everyone knew. Such was now the ambiance of the assembly that everyone joined in singing unselfconsciously.

Here is family life, thought Jane, as it was

meant to be. Why do so few attain this? It is not that this family is simple-minded, as Jane might have assumed had it been merely described to her. No, these were intelligent, knowledgeable, entertaining, and kindhearted people — not without an appreciation of culture or wit or events in the world. They had willingly fashioned this. They had deliberately made this family.

Deliberately making a family was not a concept that had occurred to Jane before. A good match was found, soon there would be children, and everything would simply fall into place, or not, rather haphazardly, she supposed, depending on circumstances. But if it could be built on purpose, truly on purpose, then this family should be the model. She was quite struck by this, and thought of it often years afterwards.

Chapter 35

The next morning, the Austens' trunks were again packed and heaved up on a coach, this time headed towards the sea at last. As they settled into their seats, a world of difference separated them. Mrs. Austen was, indeed, relieved of all her dropsy symptoms. She did not even feel a cold approaching, such was the state of her being. Mr. Austen was thinking over the many concepts of physic and theology he had discussed with the Blackall brothers. They had all recommended books to each other, and discussed theories and practical applications of their various areas of knowledge. It had been a thoroughly enlightening evening, one which Mr. Austen hoped to reciprocate at some future time.

Cassandra, for the first time since the death of Thomas Fowle, felt that particular fluttering in her chest that she had remembered from years ago. Thomas Blackall had touched her heart completely. She had never anticipated having such feelings for anyone again, and had been quite determined against it, in fact, in honor of Thomas Fowle. She had known Thomas Blackall for only for a few hours, after all. Had this happened to someone else, her advice would be to discard all such thoughts. True affection and constancy require time to develop. She would wait. They would meet again in Sidmouth in but a few weeks. Jane was also drawn to him, she knew, but this could be merely the admiration for a handsome man. In any case, there was nothing she could do except to wait.

Jane and Cassandra shared a bed chamber as they traveled. But, they had not regained that ease of talking before sleeping or early in the morning as they had in Steventon. The division that had taken place between them in Bath had left some caution. Trust and openness must now be earned through time.

Their first destination was Teignmouth, but they could view the sea long before they reached it. How glorious and fresh were the breezes passing through the coach. And, if one chose to ignore the fact of the coach, one could easily imagine being in a sail boat with crashing waves for bumps in the road. Out there, time itself drifted.

That was what Jane had hoped for: a timelessness, a release from constraints, and a long gray nothingness in which to lose herself for a time, to be a kite. But after the previous evening, the kite had found wind to propel it. She could no longer be content to simply allow time to drift.

For now there was a goal beyond Teignmouth: the Sidmouth Esplanade, the place where she would see Thomas Blackall again. Her vision of herself waiting on a stone pier now changed to waiting on the Esplanade.

This was the man she had been waiting for. This was the man with whom she would build a family, deliberately, like Dr. John Blackall's family.

Thomas had already experienced the deep love of that life and family. With these thoughts, all of Jane's anxieties about marriage and children fell away, for there was joy in such a life, the joy of creation and of purpose that had not occurred to her before. She could not be certain of Thomas' feelings after only one evening, of course, but her sense of their connection was so strong that she was quite willing to span most of the connection herself until they could meet again. She would wait. Impatiently, to be sure, but she would wait.

The coach delivered them to Teignmouth in the late afternoon, when the sun's rays slanted golden across the water. Their trunks were taken into the Thornhill Hotel, where they would reside for a few days before traveling forward to Starcross.

Their supper at the hotel that evening was remarkable for the absence of the sort of discussions held at the Blackalls supper. Had the long drive withered their interest in conversing, or was the Austen family one that could never be the Blackall family? This thought saddened Jane, for, although she felt she could see each family clearly, she could not tell what would need to be different from the Austens to create a Blackall family. This was the puzzle she tried to work out as she fell asleep.

The next days in Teignmouth brought some rain, during which the Austens visited a museum and other indoor places. But they had determined to explore each town fully, so they would wait however long until sunshine could make enjoyable an open carriage, and strolling and admiring all there was in and around the town.

On both gray days and sunny days, Jane took exercise with any of her family who would accompany her to the shore. The sea changed every day in both color and temper, much to her delight, as if it had a life of its own, which she supposed it did.

Chapter 36

The next destination was Starcross, in which the Austens spent a few more rainy days until the sun took pity upon them once more. By this time, the Austens were quite ready to travel to their final destination of Sidmouth. The anticipation of packing and unpacking their trunks, to say nothing of actually performing those operations, tended now to dampen their enjoyment of each successive town.

"Sidmouth has become very fashionable, I believe," said Mrs. Austen on the journey there. "Quite the new Bath, I understand."

"Oh, Mamma, let us hope not," said Jane.

"But my sister has said it has assembly rooms and new shops. And many fine families now have holiday homes there. And there are bathing machines."

"I do wish to try one, Mamma. What say you? Do you dare?" asked Jane.

"I cannot say. I shall decide after you tell me of your success. I would not attempt it, in any case, if my dropsy returns."

"Are they quite safe, Papa?" asked Cassandra.

"I have not heard of any danger. There is a matron, I believe, to operate it and to assist the ladies into the water. Of bathing itself, that must be conducive of health if not overindulged. It must only be tiring, I should think, as is any form of exercise."

This brought a space of silence, as they each had thoughts upon this interesting idea. Mrs. Austen, having the fewest thoughts, broke the silence.

"My dear, have you any acquaintances there whom we must meet? Or any of the Leigh-Perrot's acquaintances? I am longing for morning visits again. This lolling about all the day is very well for a short while, but I must have a little stimulation, you know."

"I can think only of the Bullers, my dear, who recommended Sidmouth," answered Mr. Austen. "But, as you say, there shall be many fine families. Undoubtedly, you shall meet them in the shops and develop some schemes or other."

"Yes, yes. But we will have been introduced to no one, you know."

"Mamma, as this is a place for holidays, very few people will have been introduced. Everyone must be strangers. Perhaps it is more easy for that reason," said Cassandra.

"We shall, at any rate, have Thomas Blackall in a week or two," said Jane. "Perhaps he has more acquaintances there."

"Undoubtedly, Jane," said Mrs. Austen. "For as renown as Dr. Blackall is, he must have a vast number of people who admire him anywhere."

"It is not he who is coming, you know, Mamma. It is his brother," said Jane.

"Oh, yes, to be sure. And not Samuel. Thomas, of course," said Mrs. Austen.

"No, Samuel had not been mentioned, Mamma. And a good thing, too, I daresay," said Jane.

"Oh, do not think ill of Samuel because he was not able to come to you, my dear. He could not help it, you know," said Mrs. Austen, now having said more than she intended.

"Was he ill, then, Mamma? What could he mean by not visiting Ashe if he had such a violent attachment to me?" asked Jane.

"He was not ill, my dear. At least I had not heard so from Madam Lefroy. I believe I can tell you now, as we can be sure of not meeting him again. He was prevented because he had taken a vow of chastity. Or celibacy. I know not which. He could not marry. It is required of all fellows at Emmanuel College."

"What?" cried Jane. "Can this be true, Mamma?"

"Madam Lefroy declares that it is. I am sorry, my dear. But perhaps solving this little mystery may help you feel less ill towards him. He could not help it. And he still feels it deeply," said Mrs. Austen.

"Oh! Poor soul. I had no great attachment to him, to be sure. But to be so tormented by a circumstance such as this...I am heartily sorry for him. Indeed I am. Did you know of this, Cassandra?"

"No, certainly. It was a mystery to me, as well, why he should suddenly disappear. Now that we know, we may sympathize."

"It is true enough that fellows of divinity at universities are required to commit themselves in this way," said Mr. Austen. "It is a test of devoutness, I believe. It is one that I cannot be equal to, however. Fortunate I am to have separate disciplines. My theological one is quite separate from my scholarly one. Therefore, I may be a vicar, a husband, a father, and a scholar at once. I would have it just so. In fact, I cannot agree that devoutness requires such a test as to make men miserable. Life, itself, is trying enough.

"I have read, although I cannot confirm it," he continued, "that the Papists decided this course in order to dispense with the idea of property heirs. It was in their own interest to prevent the creation of families and the inheritance troubles they would create."

"Papa! I am shocked!. Surely, you are mistaken," cried Jane again.

"I would not have you repeat such a story willy-nilly, of course. It must shock all who have true compassion. However, such is the faith and dedication of many men that they are willing to take such an oath. It is their calling, and they feel it keenly."

In fact, both Jane and Cassandra were shaken. Neither knew how to ask the question that was on both their minds. But both knew it must be asked, nevertheless.

"Papa, is it true of all fellows of divinity at all universities? Must they all take vows of celibacy?" asked Cassandra.

"I know not," said Mr. Austen, wrinkling his brow.

Here Jane and Cassandra could breathe only a little.

"Is Thomas Blackall in such a situation? Is he a fellow at Exeter?" asked Jane.

"He told me that he is, yes."

"And do you know whether he has taken such a vow?" asked Jane.

"It is not a question one asks of another, Jane. Do give me the credit of being a gentleman," smiled Mr. Austen.

"Yes, indeed, Jane. The very impertinence of such a question!" said Mrs. Austen.

"I beg pardon. I only wondered whether it could be the reason for his not having a family of his own. That is all. But, you are right, Papa, such a question cannot be attempted."

Chapter 37

Sidmouth was refreshing, and beautifully situated among the deep green hills. All was sunny and clean on the day they arrived, with clapboard houses in a row along the Esplanade, all freshly painted white for the season, and their awnings brightly striped.

The Austen's coach came to a halt in front of the Old Ship Inn, which was near enough to the Esplanade that a swift breeze caught the women's skirts playfully as they stepped down to the gravel.

The trunks were heaved down and into their chambers yet again, but for the last time for at least a month. Everything could now be put away properly in cupboards.

Jane and Cassandra, however, would not take the time for these proprieties, wishing instead to explore the Esplanade while there was still a beautiful light on the sea.

There were considerably more people here than in any of the other towns along the coast. But, they were pleased to discover that Sidmouth did not remind them very much of Bath. There was leisure here of a much less self-conscious sort. Less strutting for its own sake, perhaps, and an easier, more playful manner. It suited them both very much.

"This is my idea of a pleasant seaside resort," said Jane. "It is precisely as I imagined it. Only think of all the history that must be here, of the sailors' widows and children, the lonely old fishermen, the swindlers and bankers and businessmen who sought to develop this as a resort. I wonder if they are all still here, walking past us, similarly wondering whether we have interesting histories and stories of our own."

"They might be disappointed, I daresay," said Cassandra, "all things considered. Our lives have not been so very interesting. Nor are they likely to be."

"Oh, Cassandra. We may not have fortunes of our own, if that is what you mean, but our lives can be interesting, nevertheless. In Bath, less so, I grant you. But here...can you not feel it?"

This was one of the differences of their temperaments. Jane was naturally the more lively in the face of anxiety.

"Do not you think we have had an interesting holiday? Did you not think meeting the Blackall family was interesting, for example?"

"But, Jane, that constitutes observing other peoples' interesting lives, not actually living an interesting life," said Cassandra.

"I see what you mean. But having those experiences are part of what I consider as having an interesting life. Not wholly, of course, but partly. Watching others, you know, and imagining what their lives must really be like."

"You are more content, I suppose, to live life passively. You are a good watcher. And a good listener," said Cassandra. "I wish to actually have a life of my own, to have a family, and to have children. It has been my dream, you know, and I fear it may never come to pass. Not any more."

"Oh, I am sorry, Cassandra, to have reminded you of it. I would not have wished for that, especially in this place of ease and felicity. But I protest I am not content to live passively. You are quite wrong there."

"But, I have not heard you say you wished for a family of your own, for children. You must therefore live a more passive life. That is what I mean."

"But you are now wrong on both counts, Cassandra. It is true that I have not always wished for the responsibilities of marriage, of children, but many of my ideas have altered since I was younger, you know," said Jane.

"I am all astonishment! I know your feelings, even recently, about household matters. And child-bearing has always been a subject of your disdain. Do you mean to say that your opinions have now changed? What has occasioned this change?"

"Well, it is not so easy to explain. I am not at all certain that I can explain, in fact. But, I must say that I was much affected by the Blackall family. That is only the most recent example, you know. Did they not touch your heart, Cassandra? Such a family as anyone could wish for. I would overcome whatever was necessary for such a family, such a life."

"Oh, yes, I quite agree. Were they not the most charming and agreeable and…I know not all the possible descriptions that could be used. Yes, they touched my heart. Indeed. Very much so."

Neither Jane nor Cassandra was willing to take the conversation further. They decided, therefore, that they had walked far enough along the Esplanade for one day, and turned around to walk back.

Chapter 38

All the first week, the Austens walked together on the Esplanade, and took the various day excursions for which Sidmouth was now popular. To these pleasures were added thoughts of seeing all of them anew when Thomas would come. How much brighter and richer was each view, each shop, each adventure when seen through that lens. He would actually be here, walking with us, imagined Cassandra. His countenance, his amiability, his good humor would be forever attached to this place, thought Jane. Indeed, Sidmouth could not be thought to exist without either the anticipation or the presence of Thomas Blackall by either of them.

They had little interest in attending the assemblies in the evenings, however, for they knew no one. Nor did this concern them, for there would be time, after all, when Thomas would escort them.

During the second week, several new habits formed. Cassandra now found pleasure in walking on the Esplanade in the mornings with her father, rather than with Jane, for she became interested in discussing subjects related to theology with him in private. As this was the best time of the day for visiting, Jane did not like being left behind. She, therefore, walked on the Esplanade with her mother, who talked a great deal more than Jane had ears for.

One warm afternoon, Jane became

determined to try a bathing machine. She had seen other women enter the little cabins on wheels, and then seen the cabins pushed a little distance into the water for about twenty minutes, after which they returned to the shore, and the women emerged. Jane had not a bathing costume, but was told by a matron that it did not signify. Many women bathed in their chemises, and brought along dry ones. Men were not permitted in the water at the same time, preventing any lapse of modesty.

This not only seemed harmless enough, it exactly suited Jane's desire for sticking at least two toes into the sea. Possibly more. The three women went to the machines together, but only Jane found her courage. The door was closed upon her, and she felt the cabin moving into the water. When she had removed her outer clothing and shoes and stockings, she slowly opened the door at the other end, and saw that a small ladder had been placed for her to descend into the shallow water. Her eyes were wide as she came down two steps, and then she stopped. There were, perhaps, six other women already in the water, walking about and splashing. One woman had even partially submerged herself. What a spectacle!

With her right hand held by a matron, Jane descended the stairs, and placed her feet directly onto the sand under the water. What a strange sensation, watching her feet move under the water as if they were fish. She reached her hands into the cold water briefly, and decided against going any farther. This was enough for the first day. But it was a thrilling sensation to have been in the vast sea.

When they returned to the inn, they found that Thomas Blackall had come, and was now chatting happily with Mr. Austen. They both rose when the women approached, and helped them up the stairs to the little terrace.

"Why, Mr. Blackall," cried Mrs. Austen. "What a pleasure it is to see you! How came you to find us?"

"Since I did not find you on the Esplanade, I simply went from one inn to another to seek you out. Sidmouth is not grown so large that it is more than an hour's work. Do I find you all quite well and settled here?" asked Thomas.

"Oh, indeed, yes," said Mrs. Austen. "We are vastly well entertained here. And, you may be sure, all my health symptoms have gone away. I only wish I could now thank Dr. Blackall myself. But perhaps you will extend my courtesies to him when you next see him."

"Indeed, I shall. And very pleased I am to hear it."

"How long do you mean to stay, sir?" asked Mr. Austen.

"Much depends on the health of my friend. You may remember, I have come to visit him and do what I can to encourage his spirits. It may be one or two weeks. Then I must return to my duties.

"Miss Austen, Miss Jane Austen, how do you find Sidmouth?" asked Thomas.

"Quite delightful, I thank you," said Cassandra.

"The sea is a wonder, is it not, sir?" asked Jane. "I think of my brothers in the navy drifting across it somewhere between here and France, and marvel at it. It is the same sea we share."

"Under the same sun and moon," said Thomas. "We are all related, are we not?"

"We would be honored, sir, if you could join with us for tea here on the terrace," said Mr. Austen. "It would be a pleasure for me to continue the conversation we had at Dr. Blackall's home."

"Perhaps another day, sir. I would not wish to leave my friend on his own today."

"He is most welcome to join us, if he is equal to it," said Mrs. Austen.

"I wish that he were, but I fear not. Quiet and rest is what he requires, and someone to minister to him. He is an old school fellow whose health was always uncertain. He has no family. And now, in his final time, he wishes me to stay with him."

"Oh, to be sure. How good you are," said Mrs. Austen.

"It is only what I am called to do, and I do it with pleasure."

"Will you come tomorrow, Mr. Blackall, if your friend can spare you?" asked Cassandra.

"Certainly, if you wish it," said Thomas.

"That we do, for someone must minister to you, as well," said Jane.

Chapter 39

The next day, Thomas ran to catch up beside Jane and Cassandra as they walked along the Esplanade. He laughed and bent over slightly with his hands to his knees to regain his breath.

"Mr. Blackall, you frightened us!" cried Cassandra.

"We expected you later in the afternoon," said Jane. "How does your friend today?"

"He is rallying, I believe. This morning, he sat up in bed and ate a breakfast of porridge and a cup of tea. I had not expected so good a beginning to this day. His color was also much the better. He was good enough to say that it was all due to my arriving, but he is overly kind, I daresay. What a fellow is he! And what preposterous mischief we made as lads. To be with him is to become a boy a second time."

"Your memories are fond, then, of your school days?" asked Cassandra.

"No more than most boys, I imagine. Our masters were strict, and we rebelled where we could. It is, perhaps not the ideal, but the strictures encouraged our imaginations. And that is what I remember. Your father was a schoolmaster, I believe. Was he very strict with his pupils?"

"When required, to be sure," said Jane. "But his facility was such that imagination was part of the whole. Many was the time that I sat with my back against the door outside of the schoolroom in order to hear. He was kind, but his expectations were prodigious. No boy was suffered to rest his poor head for long."

"How far we have walked! Shall we return by a different way? We may see some shops or something else to amuse us," said Thomas.

They wandered through the town along new avenues, rested on benches occasionally, and looked at shop windows, ironmonger workshops, fish sellers, furniture makers, and all the wonders of the small town.

Upon returning to the inn, he sought out Mr. Austen.

"If you will permit me, sir, I would be pleased to offer tea to you and your family here at the inn. Or is it time for supper? Time has escaped me."

As the time was between the two, they determined to have tupper, their own combination of tea and supper. Thomas was particularly attentive to Mrs. Austen, inquiring after her health and how she found her new home in Bath. No detail was too small to interest him, although there was a goodly number of them.

"With Mr. Austen now retired, we cannot boast of a manor, but I flatter myself we shall be quite comfortable. Do you come to Bath often, sir? We would be vastly pleased to be honored with a visit at any time convenient. To you, I mean. Convenient to you, of course. Inconvenience to us does not signify in the least. Any time at all."

"I thank you, madam, for your kind offer. However, I know not when I may be in Bath next. My duties at Exeter are quite extensive just now. But I shall certainly write a note, if you wish it, if I see an opportunity."

"Oh, yes, indeed! We would like it above anything! A note, to be sure! And are you fond of dancing, Mr. Blackall? For Bath is quite renown for its assemblies, you know," said Mrs. Austen. "I may assure you that both of my girls are excellent dancers, are they not, Mr. Austen?"

"Certainly they are, madam. But, there are assembly rooms here in Sidmouth, as well, if they are so inclined."

"Yes, and they are quite large and well attended, I understand. I would be delighted to escort you there some evening, if you wish," said Thomas, without looking at anyone in particular.

"We would be honored, I'm sure," said Mrs. Austen.

The evening ended as it did the previous day, with good wishes all round, and the probability of meeting again the next day.

Chapter 40

Thomas did not appear the following day, however, nor was any explanation sent. Since no definite time had been agreed upon, the Austens decided that one of them, at least, must be at home throughout the day, so eager were they to receive him again. Mrs. Austen was chosen. She had made a few acquaintances on the grounds, and was not unhappy to be off her feet for the day.

Jane and Cassandra walked through the town with Mr. Austen, confident that Thomas would be waiting for them upon their return. Their eager anticipation turned to dismay, however, to discover his absence.

"Well, girls, let this remind us that we cannot produce whomever we choose whenever we wish them to appear," said Mr. Austen. "Mr. Blackall had other business, I daresay. Let us allow him discretion to use his time as he wishes. He did not absolutely declare his intention to return, after all. But, I believe he shall return, and we shall all be gratified."

"Relieved, in my case, Mr. Austen," declared Mrs. Austen. "For such a man does not disappoint easily. I only hope he has not caught the illness of his poor friend, and is likewise at death's door. Indeed, I could not bear another death as Mr. Fowle's."

"Mamma, you are too hasty. Pray, do not

distress us with such thoughts," said Jane. "What an idea."

Since the idea *had* been mentioned, however, there was a silence as each of them organized their opinions on the matter.

"I quite agree with Jane, Mamma. He has undoubtedly simply been delayed. Let us not stop our lives, or his, at this small matter. He shall return as soon as he is able."

On the following day, in the late afternoon, Thomas finally did appear at the inn, much the worse for wear. He was as gray as is humanly possible. His movements were heavy as he climbed the few stairs to the terrace and looked upon the Austens waiting for him.

Jane ran to him first.

"Thomas," she cried. "What has happened? Are you unwell? Pray, come and be seated. Here, you may have my tea."

The other three had now stood up, ready to receive him.

"I thank you. I am not ill, at least I cannot tell if I am ill. Yes, tea will be a comfort, indeed. I am heartily sorry to come to you in this manner. But I could not remain away longer. You deserve an explanation of my absence. I beg you will pardon me."

"Oh, what can be the matter? Is there nothing we can do for your present relief?" cried Cassandra.

"Nothing, I thank you. I shall explain. My friend has died. My beloved friend. He died in his sleep the evening I was here. I had hoped to administer last rites to him when his time came, but I was unable to so much as say goodbye to him. I am indeed grieved. He deserved better, to be sure."

"Oh, Thomas," said Mr. Austen. "You blame yourself for an act of God. When you left him, he seemed well enough. He was blessed with a good day before parting. You could not have predicted which day God was to choose. And, consider, your friend was made happy that you came to him, that you relived your memories. You have been a good friend, sir. Indeed, you have. Do not regret what you could not change."

"I regret that I was enjoying myself so at the time he needed me."

"But he did not. He was asleep, and in the hands of God. What would you say to a supplicant of yours in this instance, Thomas? Or rather, what would you think, since that may be different?"

"I know not. I know only that I miss him terribly."

"Of course you do, and there is no remedy for it, alas, except time and reflection. But, however, pray, do not add to your misery with guilt. You could not know. You could not guess. You are forgiven, indeed."

Here, Mr. Austen, touched his hand and bowed down as a pastor, which, at last, relieved Thomas of the few tears he had left.

"I beg pardon, sir. I am, perhaps, too much distressed to be in company. I shall return tomorrow, believe me."

"Thomas, there is no need to withdraw if you do not absolutely wish it," said Jane. "Not for our sakes, surely. I quite comprehend if you wish to be alone, but we shall be silent if it is only peace you require to have your own thoughts."

"I do not wish to throw you into this abyss with me. Let us hope for tomorrow to be a better day. I shall smile again, I promise you. But, no, I cannot stay away. If you will have me tomorrow, I shall surely come. I am quite restless now. I must walk back. It is not far. I beg pardon for distressing you."

He rose to go, with more apologies to everyone, and walked onto the lane.

"Wait, Thomas," cried Jane. "May I not accompany you? I shall be silent. You need not speak. Only allow me to..."

She realized immediately that she had breached decorum with this outburst.

Cassandra had now risen.

"Oh, Jane, can you not see he wishes to be alone? Pray, come back."

"Mr. Austen, do make her return before she creates a scene," whispered Mrs. Austen.

But Jane had already joined him, and they continued to walk.

The sun was now far into the western sky, with promise of a deep red sunset. Thomas smiled at Jane as soon as she was beside him.

They walked together on the Esplanade for a

long time in silence, listening to the seagulls cawing overhead as they headed for their roosts for the night. The crowds had thinned, and candles were being lit in the homes and inns and shops along the way. All had turned golden.

They stopped at last to look out towards the sea, to the endless expanse of life and death.

Chapter 41

Thomas did, indeed, return the next day, arriving at the inn in the early afternoon. All the Austens awaited him, fearful of how he had fared through the night. After Thomas had returned with Jane in the early evening the night before, he had appeared more composed and able to acquit himself well. But, a night alone under such circumstances must be very difficult, and a relapse could well be the result.

Not surprisingly, Jane had been as much talked of by the Austens as Thomas, for her impulsive display rankled all three of them, for differing reasons. Mrs. Austen was shocked at her lack of composure, and Mr. Austen was sorry that Thomas could not be left in peace as he had wished.

Cassandra's reasons were more complex. She was now convinced that Jane was in love with Thomas, and that Thomas did not absolutely refuse Jane's particular company. The two of them had been gone for over an hour together, a normally shocking idea, had the circumstances not allowed, at least by Mr. Austen's reckoning, for leniency.

During the times Thomas had been with them, Cassandra had been careful to observe whether he preferred the company of Jane or herself. But she could not discern a difference in his behavior, which, perhaps, a gentleman would be careful to conceal.

Thomas' countenance was much improved on this day. He brought with him a book of his own for Mr. Austen, and three scarves he had purchased in the morning for the ladies. These were handsome gifts, indeed, as judged by all the Austens.

"I am much in your debt for your forbearance last evening. Indeed, your kind words, and even silences at the right times, have brought me back to my proper state of mind. I am most grateful. I shall never forget your kindness."

"Sir, I am only gratified that we may have been able to be of some comfort to you," said Mr. Austen. "We none of us can manage through this life alone, I daresay."

"I believe you are right. I have now taken care of all I can for my poor friend and his estate. I shall leave tomorrow for Exeter, or, rather, stop at Totnes on the way there. My work cannot be delayed much longer, for the new school year begins soon. And, I do not wish to tread further upon your hospitality. But I would inquire now for the honor of returning to you soon, as I am able. Do you stay long in Sidmouth?"

"Only until September," said Mrs. Austen. "But, as I may have mentioned before, we shall eagerly anticipate a visit from you at whatever time you choose in Bath. Only name the day."

"I cannot imagine a more obliging family. You have all been so good me, a near stranger, after all," said Thomas, this time looking at Jane particularly.

"Not a stranger, sir. A friend. You are certain you cannot stay longer?" asked Mr. Austen.

"Indeed, no. My duties as Fellow at Exeter forbid it."

"I see. Do you find the responsibilities at Exeter, as a fellow, I mean, very restricting, sir? My understanding is that there are considerable differences between universities. Are there not?" asked Mr. Austen.

"I believe there are some differences, but in the main, the situations are similar. We have all declared commitment to our purpose. A vow, more correctly."

Thomas blushed a little at this, for the topic was somewhat uncomfortable just now. He was experiencing a trial of faith, he knew. One that required thought and prayer. And, as he correctly perceived that he was vulnerable at this time, with his friend's death, he dared not entirely trust to his emotions, much as he could be swept away by them. He did trust his faith, however.

"Of course," said Mr. Austen. "And that vow is perpetual, I believe?" asked Mr. Austen, blushing a little, as well.

"The vow is considered sacred. So long as I am Fellow, it must be honored."

"Ah. Just so."

"But, there have been fellows who have resigned their posts to become more secular: vicars, private chaplains, and so forth. It is not unheard of. In those cases, the vows are dissolved."

This line of conversation had now proceeded as far as anyone could bear. Mrs. Austen did not quite follow the meaning, but both Jane and Cassandra were emotionally exhausted from the experience. And, as they considered later, they were much beholden to their father for clarifying the points they longed to know.

"I shall not trespass further on your time. I must make my own arrangements. I heartily wish you a very splendid holiday," said Thomas. "I hope to communicate as soon as I can plan another time for a short holiday. In the mean time, you have every good wish of mine."

"As do we, sir. My blessings to you and your dear family. Pray, have a safe journey," said Mr. Austen.

Thomas took his leave with only a slight glance back, one that neither Jane nor Cassandra could absolutely determine whom he singled out. Jane thought it was her. And Cassandra feared that it was true.

Chapter 42

A few days later, Thomas Blackall waited outside his brother John's office of physic in Totnes, waiting for the last patient of the day to exit the door.

"Thomas, welcome. Your journey was easy, I hope. And your holiday. But, wait. Pray, let me send a note to Laura so she may expect you at supper. How good it is to see you. Now, tell me all."

It was but three in the afternoon, leaving a few hours before their presence would be anticipated at John's home.

"Come, let us repair to our local public house. A pint of ale at the end of a journey is just the thing. You shall be refreshed," said John.

"I beg you would stay," said Thomas. "For I have much to relate to you that I would not air in a boisterous public place. I require your good counsel on an important matter."

"Certainly. Certainly. Shall we take the chair home? Laura, you know, provides much better counsel than do I. And together, why, we may solve any earthly matters with very little effort!"

"Pray, may I come in to your offices? That will be the best.

"First, our friend has died, John. I knew he could not outlast his illness. He knew it, as well. We spent many happy hours in Sidmouth laughing at our follies and small triumphs at school. He was not equal to taking the waters or the sea, but we ate our meals together, and talked into the night. He was not unwilling to go, at last. He only wanted someone to talk with, to make his last days less lonely, and to be given a blessing, I believe. How proud I was of him, his courage, his willingness to surrender to his fate, to his God. What an honor for me to have been so chosen, to be called to this service I love. You can not conceive..."

Thomas wept tears he did not know he still had. There had been more tears during his journey here, but he had been determined to collect himself for his brother's sake. He could not bear to be a burden to those he loved, to weep at every turn, to cast others continually to his own melancholy frame of mind, and away from their own pleasures.

"How I thought of you, John, and wished for you to be there to guide me."

"But this is most extraordinary, Thomas. You are my older brother, after all, and you are a cleric. It seems we have traded roles since last we met."

"So it seems. But now, you do remember the Austen family, who were here at supper some weeks ago?"

"Of course. I liked them immensely. And you were to meet them in Sidmouth. How do they?"

"Very well, very well. But, John, pray, let me speak. I must confess to you...I must acknowledge that I have developed a close attachment to Miss Jane Austen, and I know not what to do. That is the reason for my coming to you. I can not reconcile my

feelings. I have a vow to uphold. John, I beseech
you, give me guidance."

"Oh, Thomas," said John, smiling. "What a
sweet dilemma. I did not know you had it in you.
You are a man of many parts, and cannot deny one
for the other, you know. All the parts exist, some
with more harmony than with others, to be sure.
But do not deny this part of yourself. Can you not
rejoice for what you feel? Is it not joy?"

"Oh, yes. It is joy. It is delirium, it is
madness," said Thomas, now also smiling.

"And Jane Austen! What a prize! What a
delight she is. Laura and I laughed for days after
she left us, for all her wit and remarkable opinions.
She is worth having, Thomas."

"She is a jewel, is she not? Oh, John, let us be
serious. Let us be practical. I must relinquish my
post, which I also love. And for which I have felt a
calling since I was a boy."

"Yes, I well remember. But, relinquishing
your current post does not mean you can no longer
be a cleric. You must choose to serve in a different
way, one which shall not have the prestige, the
scholarship, nor the wages of your current post. But,
Thomas, that is not the dilemma, for I know you
well enough to know how you would choose
among these.

"Your dilemma is your family, whom I know
you also love. It is Samuel. He has loved Jane for
these many years. His temperament is quite
different from yours, but he has struggled mightily,

as you know. At last, he made the choice to uphold his vows, which does not mean he has forgotten her. Quite the contrary, for he speaks often of her to both me and to Laura. He almost joined us for the supper you mentioned, to see her once more. But, he knew he should break his heart again.

"Thomas, if you offer Jane a declaration, our family shall be broken. Two brothers cannot love the same woman without a breech. I am sorry to say it, Thomas, for I know it will not be easy for you. But tell me, have you left Jane with an understanding from which your honor can not allow you to withdraw?"

"No, no. That I care for her, she knows, undoubtedly. But no more was discussed. I would not use her ill."

"You are not wrong to love her, Thomas, and I cannot blame you for making a decision to marry her, if you choose. It is your life to live. But your family would be broken. Samuel would be forever lost to you."

All the thoughts that had been swirling in Thomas's head for days had at last settled and become clear.

"John, I cannot deny my feelings for Miss Austen. Nor for poor Samuel. I did not fully realize before now how he must suffer. He must be forever lost, in either event. And, indeed, so must I."

Chapter 43

My dear Mr. Austen,

I send my best regards to you, honored sir, as well as to your estimable family, and hope that this letter finds you all in the best of health, and enjoying your holiday in Sidmouth.

I write to you on a matter of some delicacy. Whether it shall bring loss or indifference to you and your family, I know not. I know only that duty demands that an explanation be provided to you so you may judge of yourself the best manner of relaying the information I shall now impart.

To make short of the matter, our family finds itself in the unusual position of having two brothers very much attached to your daughter, Miss Jane Austen. Such an excess in most other circumstances must be cause for joy, indeed. In this particular case, however, it is a cause for the utmost distress.

My brothers Thomas and Samuel are both respected fellows of universities, and as such, have made solemn vows of celibacy that may only be reconsidered upon leaving their posts. These are heavy considerations, indeed, for both my brothers, as they feel their calling most devoutly.

Some years ago, you may already know, Samuel made the decision, after extensive prayer, to honor his vow, and to give up all considerations of extending an offer of marriage to Miss Jane. While he does not reconsider that decision at this time, he cannot but be grieved at the thought of what he has left behind him.

Thomas's decision regarding this matter differs. Upon reflection and discussion with me this past week, he feels he can serve his calling in a more secular way satisfactorily if it means he could win the acceptance of Jane. He is quite prepared to do so, were it not for one additional factor: he loves his brother Samuel. For Thomas to be accepted by Jane would mean the eternal misery of Samuel. After long and uneasy conversations together upon this subject, we are now both convinced that to begin a new life under such a heavy cloud cannot be attempted with honor, nor with joy. His family would be breeched forever. Therefore, he shall not attempt it.

To be sure, I know little of what your perceptions have been upon this matter, or what your feelings must now be. I shall leave it to your own discretion how much or how little of this to convey to your family.

I shall only say that Thomas has given his approbation to the writing of this letter to you. He wishes to pay his respects and gratitude for the hospitality your family has shown to him. We have agreed that Samuel should not be advised of this matter, for it would only add to his heartache.

I write this letter myself so that any communication to be made regarding this matter might be forwarded to me rather than to either of my brothers, and to assure you, dear sir, that I remain

> your humble and most obedient servant,
> Dr. John Blackall, Totnes

Such was the news on a sad day in Sidmouth for Mr. Austen near the end of the family's holiday. He knew not how best to proceed, except that he must dispose of the letter immediately before Mrs. Austen becomes aware of its existence. He, therefore, determined to take a solitary walk on the Esplanade, during which he tore the letter into many pieces and buried them into a barrel of refuse. That could not be the end of the matter, of course, for he knew that both his daughters were much attracted to Thomas, and would eagerly anticipate a future visit. To end the speculation now must be a greater mercy than to allow them to wait in vain. To explain the truth of the matter must also be injurious to them both.

Cassandra would undoubtedly feel a double pain, that of discovering that her feelings had not been reciprocated, and that they had been granted to her sister, instead. And, Jane would be devastated to know the conditions under which her future happiness had been cut off. Indeed, her temper was such that she might well continue to wait in vain, discounting any future opportunities for happiness. This was a torment to all, but it must be solved somehow.

After tea, then, in private, Mr. Austen began.

"I received a sad communication today, that we must all grieve. Indeed, it pains my heart to relay to you its contents, but I can think of no alternative. Mr. Thomas Blackall has met with an accident on his return, and has died. We shall see him no more. We can but pray for his soul. And for his dear family. Indeed, I am very, very sorry. My heart is broken, for my own sake as well as for all of yours. We all esteemed him greatly."

"No, Papa, say no more!" cried Cassandra. "No, I cannot bear it. Not again! Must the gentlemen I regard be fated to die? Sir, can you not be mistaken? Oh, Jane."

Cassandra trembled, and looked to Jane for she knew not what. But Jane could only look down, so lost was she. Had Thomas done himself a mischief over his guilt towards his friend? A guilt which would not permit joy? Her tears began at his torment. And at the senseless loss. Had her own ability to help him see a future beyond his guilt been more adequate, this would surely not have been the result. He had abandoned their future, their happy family. It was never to be. She was alone again. God, have mercy on his soul. He was too good.

"Oh, my girls!" cried Mrs. Austen. "What can be done? Oh, what a dear gentleman. Gone! I cannot believe it. He was to come to us in Bath. And now he shall not come at all! It has all come to nothing! I call that very bad luck, indeed!"

Chapter 44

The sea and the clouds, how changeable, how malleable by the observer, thought Jane. The soft puffs of white now near to gray, casting shadows over the innocent rippling water.

Mr. Austen accompanied Jane this day, for she did not want Cassandra's company just now. And not her mother's, certainly. They walked up to the top of Peak Hill and looked out.

"Another perspective, my dear," said Mr. Austen.

"And yet the same reality, Papa."

"The world is larger than we are."

"But we are still only who we are, able to see only what is before us, what our senses tell us, what we feel. We feel too much, for knowing as little as we do."

She was glad to spend time with her father now, for he knew when to be silent, when to simply let her speak, and when to give her encouragement. And when none of those was useful, when to support her faith.

"I long to return to Bath, Mr. Austen," said Mrs. Austen. "Oh, to go to the theater, to the assemblies, the pump rooms. We are in want of society. When shall we return?"

"I can settle accounts here quickly. If you wish, we may leave in, say, two days. Will that suit everyone?"

"Yes, Papa, I long to be gone," said Cassandra. "I am quite tired of Sidmouth for one year."

"I am, as well," said Jane. "The drawback, of course, is that it is Bath to which we must escape. But, perhaps we are meant to be constantly escaping from one place to another like bees."

"No, indeed. We shall be quite comfortable in Bath," said Mrs. Austen.

"Shall you be comfortable in Bath, Cassandra?" asked Jane.

"For a time, I believe so. It is as good a spot as any. It is not home, however. I shall never again have a home. And none of my own, to be sure."

"How can you say so, Cassandra?" asked Mrs. Austen. "You are not a spinster, yet. You have quite some good years before you."

"For what purpose, I cannot say," said Cassandra. "I do not hope for an attachment, or a family now. That is all over. But, I am quite attached to Edward's children, you know. I am fortunate to be an aunt. How I love them!" she said, with a small break in her voice.

Later that evening, Jane and Cassandra talked alone for the first time since they learned of Thomas's death. They had, in fact, avoided the difficult subject.

"Are you in earnest, Cassandra? Have you really resigned yourself to be a spinster? I cannot believe it of you."

"But we are different, you and I. You are

more resilient in these matters, where I am devastated. I simply choose never to undertake this miserable business again. I wish to remember Thomas Fowle as my fiance. Thomas Blackall, was, after all, never mine. That was plain enough. And you, running after him in the night…I shall never forget the sight. No, I am now resigned. My capacity for pain has been reached."

"Oh, Cassandra. I did not wish you pain. Truly. Pray do not wish it upon me."

Cassandra had not intended to make this exclamation, but now that it had been made, the aftermath looked bleak to them both. How was such a breech to be mended?

Chapter 45

As anticipated, the rooms at Sydney Place in Bath provided little of the comfort either of the Miss Austens required. They found Bath diversions mildly amusing, to be sure, but nothing more. They could not take exercise without escorts, and there were no private country lanes close by. Privacy, taken for granted formerly in the barns and courtyards and fields of Steventon, could not now be found. Their world was constricted, and their days increasingly spent in conversation with their mother, or with each other. And there could be no day's escape to their friends at Ashe Rectory or Manydown.

The object of Mr. and Mrs. Austen's prolonged stay in Bath became increasingly clear to Jane and Cassandra. Their primary object was to find husbands for their daughters, and they would all remain until that was accomplished.

After Christmas, however, observing that their daughters had not recovered well from the Sidmouth incident, the Austens permitted Cassandra to go to her brother Edward for an extended visit. Jane thereafter wrote a letter to Catherine Bigg, asking for permission to come to Manydown, which was heartily granted. Lovelace Bigg-Wither, ever gallant and generous, sent his carriage to retrieve her in early January.

It was at Manydown that Jane found peace

again. Almost a year ago, she had looked at the snow through these same library windows, and Mr. Bigg-Wither had been sitting in his same comfortable chair.

"We have missed you, Jane. Indeed, we are sorry that you cannot love Bath, but it is hardly surprising. To those, like us, who have been born and bred in the country, city life cannot charm. It does not fill those souls who need to wander through the lanes in solitude."

"Sir, you comprehend all. I cannot be content elsewhere but in the country or at the seaside. Only those two. Preferably both."

"Jane, would it not be splendid to spend every winter here and the summer there?" asked Catherine. "That is my idea of perfection. Perhaps several days in Bath on the way for some amusement, but that is all. What say you?"

"I quite like your idea. I could earn my keep by becoming your gardener, perhaps. Cooking is quite out of the question, you know. Let me see. Ah, my embroidery, I flatter myself, is without equal. My pianoforte is but middling. But, could not a situation be cobbled together to keep my body and soul together?"

Everyone laughed. This was the old Jane.

"I do not really require rescuing, however. What I want is only the country and money of my own. I wish to pay my own way in the world: to travel in a carriage for which I have paid, to be at leisure to write as I wish, and to sell my writing, if anyone will publish it."

"You don't say, Jane!" said Mr. Bigg-Wither. "Your ambitions are grand, indeed. Pray, should you not feel immodest at such notoriety?"

"Perhaps at first, but not for long. Fanny Burney has done it, and so has Mary Wollstonecraft. I must live somehow, and if I can live by my own wits, I should be gratified, indeed. Are you very shocked, sir?"

"To be sure, I do not know the ladies of whom you speak, so I know not whether to be shocked. I suppose I am a little, for it is rather unheard of, is it not? What would society become if its women abandoned their husbands and children and homes to shut themselves up in their rooms by themselves? Only think how we must suffer!"

"La!" cried Harris in the corner. "What is t-t-two hours of p-p-peace in a day, if it makes her happy? Do you not enjoy t-t-two hours of p-p-peace in a day, sir? Does society d-d-disintegrate without you?"

"Why, Harris," laughed Jane. "Perhaps it is more accepted now than in the past."

"I suppose you mean that I am old-fashioned, my dear," said Mr. Bigg-Wither. "But if I am, I do not wish to be. I am not so very shocked by ladies writing, after all. I mean only that others could be, you know. But it may not be very likely, now that I think on it."

"It does not signify very much," said Jane. "If a little fame brings a horde to my door, I shall simply shut myself up in my room again."

A servant now brought a letter to Mr. Bigg-Wither.

"Oh, my dears! What do you think? We must go to Lizzy directly. Come, come! Heathcote has been shot!"

The carriage was readied as quickly as possible, and they sped through the snow and the lanes in the most desperate alarm.

Alas, by the time they arrived, Lizzy was sobbing over the lifeless body of her husband, accidentally shot while hunting. Heathcote, all goodness and wisdom, was dead at age thirty, leaving behind his wife and one-year-old son.

A few days later, Mr. Bigg-Wither stood to give the eulogy at the funeral, during which he attempted to portray the depth of Heathcote's character, his piety, his benevolence...but he was not equal to it. Indeed, such a man, how could there be such another? He wished God had taken himself, instead. He had lived a full enough life. But Heathcote! Too young, too young. Oh, God, how our faith is tested.

At last, Jane bowed down and wept. She wept in the church, on the return to Manydown, and deep into the night. She wept for Heathcote, for Lizzy, for little Willie, for Mr. Bigg-Wither, for Catherine, for herself, for Thomas Blackall, for Cassandra. All, all thrown into despair by death.

Where was the beauty now in creating a family, deliberately or otherwise? It was insupportable. All would be shattered, to be utterly undone. She had been naive to think of marriage and children. Only consider the sorrow that can never be repaired. Look at beautiful little Willie, playing innocently as if life is not one brutal loss after another.

Chapter 46

The following month, in April of 1802, Mr. Bigg-Wither, now resigned that Jane could not accept him if he should make her an offer, made use to her again of his carriage to transport her back to Bath.

Rushing forward now, the cool spring air brought sensations of the natural world towards her, as she remembered from childhood journeys. Moldering leaves, wet bark, chirping redwings, fallen branches, and the occasional warm breeze from somewhere beyond, from some future summer, perhaps.

She had not taken all her manuscripts with her to Manydown. *First Impressions,* which she had renamed *Pride and Prejudice,* and *Elinor and Marianne,* which she had renamed *Sense and Sensibility,* were resting in Bath. But her new novel, *Northanger Abbey,* as she renamed the original *Susan,* had been her constant companion for several years. While much of the novel took place in Bath, she could not find sufficient peace of mind there to write. She only took notes there, and then wrote the novel while in the country at Manydown.

She took up the manuscript now within the carriage, and reread what she had lately written. When would she complete it? Perhaps in Dawlish, the intended holiday place for this summer. Would she find sufficient peace there? Indeed, she longed for the sea more than ever, but was unable to separate thoughts of Thomas Blackall from the waves and the Esplanade. The Dawlish plan would cure her, would teach her to separate them. Never would she be so foolish as to become attached to another elegant gentleman at the seashore, any more than at Bath.

Her life, her heart, every sign now told her that she had merit of her own. She belonged to herself. Not to anyone named Tom, not to the Bigg-Withers, not to Cassandra, not to the rest of her family. She loved them all, but she was not them, and she would move forward as herself.

It was, at last, in Dawlish that she spoke openly to Cassandra, for the ghost of Thomas Blackall was in need of being banished for them both.

"The clouds making shadows over the sea puts me much in mind of Sidmouth," said Cassandra one day. "We were quite fortunate in the weather, do you recall? On fine days, the few clouds overhead bore no significance to the sea. But on grayer days, the lower clouds seemed almost menacing, as if they had power over the waves."

"Indeed, we are much more contented here," answered Jane, "even on gray days. Dawlish is the more comforting, with much less to distress our minds and spirits. We were both under a spell in Sidmouth. And we were both shockingly awakened from it. I regret all the pain. Well I remember it, for it lives with me still. How do you manage it?"

"Very well on most days, I believe. But I had determined years ago never to encourage such an attachment again, you know. My pain is therefore double what it might have been. Attachment mixed with guilt."

"Oh, Cassandra, pray do not torment yourself. Do you not recall father's quote of Thomas Jefferson: 'The Earth belongs to the living'?"

"No more Toms, Jane, I beg of you," laughed Cassandra. "We have had quite our share between us."

"But, all our Toms are now gone," said Jane. "Fowle, Lefroy, and Blackall. Let us now take an active part in banishing them, at last, so we may live our lives. They would not wish, certainly, to so disrupt our destinies. None of them would. Of Lefroy, I cannot be certain, but it does not signify. I now banish his ghost."

"Oh, I cannot banish Tom Fowle's ghost, Jane. You must know that. He was an honorable man, and I loved him dearly. Banish? No. Never."

"Very well. Banish him not. But live with him lightly, not as a ghost, then, but as an angel who wishes you happiness."

"Well I know that *you* are the angel, Jane. It is you who wishes me happiness. I am truly sorry we were cross in Sidmouth. I have regretted it since. Perhaps we were both under a spell, as you say. Shall we not be sisters now? You in your way, and I in mine? We are no longer children, after all."

Chapter 47

At the end of October, Jane and Cassandra were invited to spend a month in Steventon with James and Mary, and, thereafter, two or three weeks at Manydown. This would be another pleasant escape from Bath, which they both sought whenever opportunities presented themselves. And, in this instance, Jane and Cassandra were together to face James and Mary residing in the Steventon Rectory, their beloved home

"You are very welcome, my dears," said James, as his sisters descended from their carriage. "Your journey, I hope was pleasant. Capital weather we are having. Pray come inside. I long to know what you think of what Mary has accomplished in redecorating the rectory. She is a marvel, you know."

"I like the new colors, Mary," said Jane, as she walked in the front door. "Fresh and new." She had determined to be as pleasant as possible to Mary for James' sake, and because they were to be there for a full month.

"Hello! Yes, I believe these are the more fashionable colors now," said Mary cheerily. "The old ones were rather dreary, after all, were not they? I don't suppose you chose those colors, so you will not mind me saying so."

"Oh, not at all. Quite right, I did not choose them. Cassandra did."

"They had faded, no doubt, Mary," said Cassandra, recovering nicely from Jane's first mischief. "It does not signify. The effect pleases me very much. And, oh, you have removed an entire wall here. Oh!"

"It was in the way, you know. Now the children can run in a circle continuously. La! What an effect such a change can make in their happiness. They never tire of it, I assure you."

That Mary would have made alterations to Steventon Rectory had, indeed, been anticipated. However, the removal of an entire wall had not been considered, and required a few moments of adjustment to overcome.

"It is no longer our home," sighed Cassandra later in her and Jane's old bed chamber.

"Oh, I have given it up," said Jane. "I shall never forget how it was when it was ours, but houses have lives, too, I suppose, and we must not hold them back from their destinies."

One month in Steventon Rectory did not bring it back to being theirs, alas. Mary was firmly the head of the household, and made all decisions regarding who was to feed the chickens, who was to sweep the courtyard, who was to bring in water, and who was to make tea and toast. And yet, Jane found that her strengthened resolve allowed her to enjoy her days there, and to remember details from her childhood: the small window pane with the corner crack, the garden post with the hole just large enough for a small finger, and the spider web above the barn door, now supporting a new spider family, perhaps.

On November 25th, the long-familiar Bigg-Wither carriage arrived, at last, to bring Cassandra and Jane to Manydown again.

"I am not sorry to leave this place, Cassandra, though I am ashamed to admit it. It has not been two years, but already I feel myself changed forever."

Chapter 48

Catherine and Lizzy both came along in the carriage to Steventon.

"Oh, how we have missed you both!" cried Catherine. "Cassandra, it has been far too long. We must have a long chat, you know. Just look at us sitting here, four grown women. I well remember how we played around the carriage when we were children. How very odd to consider it now.

"Had I been asked those many years ago what I would conjecture about us today, I would have said we should all be handsomely married. But, here we are without any men in the carriage. What do you make of it? Are we extremely lucky or extremely unlucky?

"I beg pardon, Lizzy. You are the exception, of course. Pray, do not be angry with me."

"No, it is quite alright. I would say for myself that I am both: lucky to have been married to William, and unlucky to have lost him so soon. But lucky again to now have little Willie."

"And I," said Cassandra, "have been unlucky. But, I deserve no pity, for I am well content, I assure you. My life is as I wish it to be."

"As for me, I cannot say," said Catherine. "I am now seven and twenty, you know, which is the age at which one is generally regarded as a spinster. But I do not mind it in the least. There shall always be widowers, I suppose, who may be interested in a woman never married and without children. But I care not either way. I am perfectly content."

"Like Cassandra," said Jane, "I have been unlucky. And like Catherine, I am seven and twenty. But I am not so sanguine as either of you. I should say, rather, that I rebel at the notion of being thought a spinster, as if that is so very bad. It is only bad if there is a very small income, you know. That is the material point. I do not so much mind the former, but I greatly mind the latter. I should consider myself fortunate, indeed, if I had an income of my own, for that would provide the freedom to choose. And I mean to do it."

"Do you, indeed?" asked Catherine. "Have you then decided absolutely to write?"

"Oh, I believe I shall always write, but that will not secure an income. I must be published so people will buy my books. My brothers shall not be burdened for my care after father is gone, nor for Cassandra's. I would not like for this to be generally known, however, for I must consider first how to accomplish it, and, perhaps, how to conceal my identity. But I shall attempt it. You may depend upon it."

"That is quite a brave plan, Jane," said Lizzy. "Would it not be wiser to exert yourself further in Bath, instead? Subscribe to all the assemblies and balls, and so forth? Or, perhaps, do both? Would it not be jolly to have an income of your own to offer a husband?"

"No, it would not, Lizzy, for I would then

lose it to him. No, it must be my own. If I have earned it, I shall do with it as I please."

How good it seemed to all to have the Austens again for the holiday season. The snow, the cozy library, the familiar rooms and halls and smells from the kitchen. And this time, even Cassandra was there. And little Willie was a delight. Jane wanted for nothing. How good life was here. Like Steventon had been, but now better.

Mr. Bigg-Wither, now one and sixty years old, had overcome an illness several years ago. Although he was quite well now, he had developed a routine of retiring early in the evenings, leaving the others to manage their own entertainments. This they did quite happily.

Little Willie was the general favorite of everyone's after supper, for he had only a half hour before his own bedtime. In order not to over-exert him before sleep, he was propped up on the sofa with sofa cushions, and everyone took turns reading to him from his infant books. There were fairy stories and little morality fables and silly poems. When it was Jane's turn, she made up stories that included a little boy named Willie going off on adventures, always coming home quite tired and ready for sleep until the next day's adventures.

Then, after Willie was put to bed, Jane, Cassandra, Catherine, Harris, Lizzy, and Alethea played at cards, played piano, sang, read, and wrote letters until their own bedtimes.

This pleasant evening rhythm continued

quite contentedly for some days, with Jane finding peace for reading and writing during the day.

One evening, the subject of how long Jane and Cassandra would be staying was discussed. Two or three weeks had been originally mentioned, but this meant that they would spend Christmas in either Bath or in Manydown, depending on which they chose.

"Do your parents wish particularly for you to be in Bath for Christmas?" asked Catherine.

"I do not believe so," said Cassandra. "Some of my brothers will be there to keep them entertained. Do we have any particular reason to return to Bath before Christmas?" Cassandra asked Jane.

"None that I know of, particular or otherwise. But, perhaps your father has plans where we would be in the way. We do not wish to overstay, certainly."

"Not at all. Quite the contrary, I assure you. He had been planning to ask you to stay longer, if it were possible. He even mentioned until spring." said Lizzy.

"I should like that, m-myself," said Harris. "I quite like your s-s-stories, Jane. And I remember that you do not write well in B-B-Bath. Pray, stay until C-C-Christmas, at least. Do. And Cassandra, as well. We shall all be q-q-quite jolly, as we are now. Say you will."

"I shall write to my father to confirm it, then, if you are quite sure," said Cassandra.

"Through spring, then?" asked Catherine. "We do consider you such a part of our family, you know."

This was, perhaps, a reference to an earlier time, several years ago when Catherine thought it could have been possible for Jane to marry her father. Jane had hoped that the idea had been given up, but perhaps it was not yet entirely extinguished.

"Catherine, you cannot conceive how very grateful I am for your hospitality all these years," said Jane. "This has been a second home to me. And, in the last few years, with all the dreadful upheavals, this place, this country, this family, has been my salvation. You are all as dear to me as is Cassandra. Indeed, you are all my family. But I cannot simply move in, you know, much as I dislike Bath. I must go home eventually."

"But, if you would write and be published, as you have declared, is not Manydown the ideal? Your peace will be protected here, and we are so remote, the hordes may never find you." said Lizzy. "If you like the seaside, you may certainly go. We shall be happy to accompany you. Only think how exciting it would be!"

Jane now looked at Cassandra for guidance. Was there another scheme here? Jane had told Cassandra in the past that it seemed the Bigg-Withers were interested in a closer connection with her, and had inquired in a round-about way whether she could accept an offer from Mr. Bigg-Wither. She still could not.

"Cassandra, can we not persuade you? You take holidays away from Bath with your brother, I believe, and are fond of children. Little Willie must be your inducement here. Is he not an angel?"

"He is, indeed. But I must now protest that, although Jane and I are deeply grateful to you all, we cannot consider your suggestions as serious. We have a home, we have a family whom we love, and we have activities and plans to be with them. They must be our first consideration, to be sure."

Cassandra placed some emphasis on her words as indication that the subject should be ended for the evening. No further words could have any other effect than exasperation. There was, therefore, a short period of quiet.

"I am afraid that we have made the Austens quite weary with our haranguing. Let us say no more on the subject. There is no urgency, after all," said Lizzy. "I, for one, am eager to retire. I shall bid you all a good night."

And so did they all. That is, they wished each other a good night. Not everyone, however, was able to accomplished it.

Chapter 49

Jane was almost at the first landing of the stairs when Harris caught her attention.

"Jane, may I have a w-w-word? I believe I owe you an explanation."

They came back down the stairs and walked into the parlor.

"My family have been s-s-solicitous on my behalf, Jane. I am sorry that I did not speak s-s-sooner, myself. I had not the confidence. Indeed, I s-s-still do not, but I must now act.

"Jane, you have been my heart's d-d-desire for all my life. My only desire. My sisters have known of this, and have tried to encourage you to stay this time on my behalf, as well as on their own. They are s-s-so good, I do not d-d-deserve it.

"I am now a man, and so must speak as a man. I am one and twenty. You are, I believe, s-seven and twenty. Two years ago, the six years' difference would have been insupportable. But now, at last, it may be acceptable to you.

"My attachment to you is very strong, Jane, and I ask whether you can accept me. As I am. I am, perhaps, not handsome, nor do I flatter myself that I have your knowledge of literature or other arts. But I will try, Jane. I hardly deserve you, but you have my solemn word that I shall do whatever is in my p-power to make you as happy as you make me. Every day. May I c-continue to hope, Jane?"

"Indeed, I know not how to answer. I am deeply flattered by such an earnest offer, to be sure. I have not perceived any particular attention before, and so have not had time to consider. I am quite shocked, in fact."

"Oh, I comprehend you entirely. Indeed, the fault is mine, to be sure. You need not r-respond absolutely this evening, of course. I only ask that you would c-consider my offer.

"I may, perhaps, also add that financial consideration does not s-signify in the least. You must know that I am heir to Manydown, and have no wish to inconvenience your family's fortunes. You and I shall have all we need, I daresay, and m-more. Your sister, Cassandra, and your p-parents shall want for nothing. We shall have homes here for them, if they choose. Upon marriage, you shall also be heir to Manydown, of course, for so I shall stipulate in my will."

Since there was still silence, he continued.

"You may write and publish whatever you choose. I shall n-never attempt to dissuade you from those efforts, for I see that they make you happy. And, any earnings from their publication shall be yours entirely. Indeed, I do not wish to profit from your efforts. I wish only to be by your side, Jane."

Her eyes were now quite wide.

"In addition, I should add, I have seen your goodness with little Willie. He would be your nephew, you know. I believe I would be an ardent f-father, Jane, as well, for my models have been my own father and Heathcote, both of whom no one could f-fail to admire."

"Oh, Harris. You need not continue in this manner. I am not silent in order to increase your discomfort. Pray, believe me. I am simply astonished at your declaration, your generosity, your thoughtfulness towards me and my parents and sister."

They talked together thus for perhaps another fifteen minutes while the rest of the family had retired.

Although Harris did not require an absolute answer on this evening, Jane felt there could be no occasion for him to be made any more miserable than he had been for so long, now that he had gained the courage to make the offer.

And so, Jane had been given another chance at family and fortune. She now brought to mind her earlier desires for a family of her own, shaped and grown with deliberation, with spirit, intelligence, proper manners, joy. Above all, she wished for her children to know joy.

She would inherit a fortune and one of the handsomest and oldest manors and estates in the country. Of all this she would be mistress. If she did not choose to write, it was no longer a pressing concern, for her fortune was made. And so was Cassandra's and her parents'.

"May I continue to hope, Jane? Pray, say yes, for I know not how I shall l-live if you do not say yes."

"Then I *shall* say yes. I shall be proud to be your wife. You have done me and my family a great honor, indeed."

Chapter 50

Harris bent down to kiss Jane's hand outside of her bed chamber.

"Oh, how we shall all c-celebrate tomorrow," said Harris. "Only think how happy we will make everyone. You shall have new s-sisters, a new nephew, and a new f-father, all of whom adore you. You and I shall build an extraordinary life, Jane, and many shall benefit."

"Indeed, I am entirely overwhelmed! It is what every woman dreams of, to be sure. A new family, and Cassandra and my parents to be made safe. You are very good, Harris, and I am deeply indebted. Indeed I am."

Jane closed her door quietly, and went to her bed. For this visit, she and Cassandra did not share a bed chamber, leaving her with her own dizzying thoughts. She could barely organize them.

Should she wake Cassandra? Was it proper to accept a declaration without Mr. Austen's blessing? Or Mr. Bigg-Wither's? Should the announcement therefore wait until approbation could be sought? When would they marry? Where would they live? At Manydown? Surely, yes. That much could be safely assumed. What else? Should she return to Bath, or not? How well does the name Jane Bigg-Wither sound? How would she purchase wedding clothes? These were some of the questions quickly rising.

Once in bed, however, there were others. What would Cassandra think of the marriage? Would she feel resentful as the only spinster? The older one left behind? How happy her mother would be! And her father! To think at last she could give them some comfort on the matter of "what shall become of the girls."

How remarkable was the difference between her life only one hour ago compared to now. It was like a fairy story, where the poor urchin is discovered at last by her prince charming, for whom she had been dreaming.

Of course, Jane had not been dreaming of a prince charming. She had quite given up that childish notion. Nor would she have dreamt of someone like Harris. How did Harris compare to Thomas Blackall? Oh, there were many differences. Harris was not handsome, certainly. His manners were often trying. His stuttering could not be helped, of course, so that could not be a consideration. His health was often indifferent. His interests…what were his interests, exactly? Perhaps this was an unfair comparison.

How, then, would Harris compare to Mr. Heathcote, to set a disinterested comparison? Less pious, to be sure. Untested honor. Less mature, as well, but he could not be blamed for his age. What else? Less knowledge and education, for Mr. Bigg-Wither did not believe Harris would particularly benefit from it.

Well, to state the obvious, Harris was rich. Or

would be rich. That was in his favor. What else? It was no good comparing him to Heathcote, after all. Heathcote had been exceptional.

How, then, did Thomas Blackall compare to Heathcote? Ah! Jane had been in love with Thomas Blackall, therefore comparisons did not signify. She would have married him regardless of how he compared to anyone else.

Alas, Jane's over-logical analysis could not give her comfort. She tried mightily to discover a reason to marry Harris aside from his wealth. There was none. That was the only advantage, then. Were there any disadvantages?

What if Harris changed his mind about allowing her to write after they were married? And, could she abide married intimacy with someone she did not love? If so, would she be of the same character as Charlotte Lucas in *Pride and Prejudice*? She did not love Harris, certainly. But could she abide him until she did? What if she never did? And then died in childbirth? Why had that question not materialized when considering Thomas Blackall? Perhaps because love overrode it.

Yes, love overrode it. And a lack of love could not now justify it.

"Cassandra, are you awake? Cassandra! I must speak to you directly. It cannot wait until morning!"

At dawn, both Cassandra and Jane had their trunks packed and ready to be put on the carriage. Mr. Bigg-Wither, thank goodness, was not an early riser. He must be spared this disgrace in his home as long as possible. But Harris must be told, of course.

Harris was soon found in happy discourse with his sisters in the dining room.

"Oh, Jane, how happy you have made all of us!" cried Catherine, running towards her. "My own sister! And Cassandra, you cannot conceive…"

"Harris, I must ask for a word in private," said Jane somberly.

"Indeed, I know not whether you can ever forgive me, Harris. We cannot be married. My feelings are not the same as yours, and they may never be. I am so dreadfully sorry. I was carried away last evening by the wonderful prospects, by the courage of your declaration, and, I suppose, by flattery. I am ashamed, as well, to admit that I was unduly influenced by the benefits to me and my family your situation could provide. I am heartily ashamed for it."

"P-Perhaps you need more time to consider, Jane. Can we not discuss your apprehensions? Perhaps something could be d-done. I shall.."

"Harris, it can never be. Pray, believe me. I must now ask once more for your goodness in supplying Cassandra and me with your carriage to Steventon. We cannot stay. Surely this is plain enough. The longer we stay, the more distress this circumstance will create."

"If you wish it, certainly. Only, pray do not say never. It is too long a time. Jane, I shall always hope. Indeed, I shall."

"The carriage is at the door, Jane. Come away," said Cassandra.

"Jane, will you permit me and Lizzy to come with you as far as Steventon? You must be distressed, I know, but so are we, and we wish to amend what is possible before we lose you. We cannot bear to lose you forever," said Catherine.

Since the journey to Steventon would be short, and since the carriage was theirs, after all, Jane accepted their company.

The carriage was now filled with four women weeping instead of four women smiling. But a sort of peace was settled upon by the time the rectory came into view, and all acknowledged that friendship of such a long duration should not be severed.

"Jane, Cassandra, we did not expect you." said Mary at the door. "Your trunks...do you mean to stay? James, your sisters are at the door again."

"James, you must drive us to Bath immediately. There can be no dispute. I cannot explain. No, we are not ill, but it is urgent that we depart immediately," said Jane.

"What can be the meaning of this?" asked Mary. "James must prepare his sermon for Sunday. He cannot simply take orders from his sisters on a whim."

"He can, and he shall," said Jane. "James, we offer you no choice. We shall explain on the way. But we cannot tarry. We can no longer stay here."

All imagined the journey to Bath would be a long and miserable affair. There was weeping, of course. But James was as patient and as sweet as he had always been.

After all the tears and explanations came silence. James took Jane's hand, at last, and said, "It is difficult to know what to say in these circumstances to comfort you, Jane. However, had I been there, I certainly would not have been shocked in the least. In fact, I can assure you that I would not have accepted Harris's offer, either."

A smile crept across Jane's face. "Oh, James. How we have changed in these seven years. Or rather, how we have grown into our destinies."

Looking out of the carriage window at the wide landscape as far as she could see, she thought, *let me never again doubt it.*

Afterword

The Prime of Miss Jane Austen is a work of fiction. Although most of the events actually took place, and most of the characters are real, sufficient gaps exist in Jane Austen's biography to encourage conjecture. The gaps exist largely because Cassandra Austen destroyed many of the letters between her and Jane, especially during those circumstances the family may not have wished to be made public.

Readers interested in learning more about Jane Austen and the people in her life are encouraged to read her extant letters and any of her numerous biographies.

Since the main characters are all real, they had lives beyond the years covered in this novel. The following are summaries of their remaining years. For more information about each of them, Internet searches can provide fuller details and portraits.

Thomas Langlois Lefroy became Lord Chief Justice of Ireland. He married Mary Paul in Ireland after his law studies ended in London, and never saw Jane Austen again.

Alethea Bigg never married.

Catherine Bigg married at age thirty-three.

Elizabeth (Bigg) Heathcote never remarried.

Sir William Heathcote (little Willie) succeeded his uncle to become 5th Baronet of

Hursley, and inherited the Hursley estate.

Reverend Lovelace Bigg-Wither never remarried.

Harris Bigg-Wither married two years after proposing to Jane Austen, and inherited the Manydown estate.

Dr. John Blackall became well known in England as a specialist in dropsy and diagnosis.

Reverend Samuel Blackall resigned as Fellow of Emmanuel College in 1812, became a vicar, and married in 1813.

Reverend Thomas Blackall resigned as Fellow of Exeter in 1815, and became vicar of Tardebigg. No record of a marriage can be found.

Cassandra Austen never married.

Jane Austen never married. Instead, she became one of England's greatest novelists.